*"So ju
bodygu*

O'Halloran's gaze locked with hers. Her heart slammed against her chest as he held the door and stepped inside the elevator. As one big hand cupped her jaw, she acknowledged that somehow she had managed to completely misread the situation.

His head dipped. She had a fractured moment to log the masculine scents of soap and skin, the heat blasting off his body. His mouth brushed hers once, twice, then settled more firmly.

Heat and sensation shot through her as he angled her jaw to deepen the kiss. A split second later, O'Halloran released her and stepped back out into the hall.

He hit the close button. "Honey, who do you think is guarding you? I am."

Dear Reader,

We have exciting news for you! Starting in January, Harlequin Romantic Suspense is unveiling a brand-new look that's a fresh take on our beautiful covers. Turn to the back of the book for a sneak peek.

There's more! Along with new covers, the stories will be longer—more action, more excitement, more romance. Follow your beloved characters on their passion-filled adventures. Be sure to look for the newly packaged and longer Harlequin Romantic Suspense stories wherever you buy books.

In the meantime, you can check out this month's adrenaline-charged reads:

CHRISTMAS CONFIDENTIAL by Marilyn Pappano and Linda Conrad

COLTON SHOWDOWN by Marie Ferrarella

O'HALLORAN'S LADY by Fiona Brand

NO ESCAPE by Meredith Fletcher

Happy reading!

Patience Bloom

Senior Editor

FIONA BRAND

O'Halloran's Lady

HARLEQUIN®
entertain, enrich, inspire™

Recycling programs
for this product may
not exist in your area.

ISBN-13: 978-0-373-27803-9

O'HALLORAN'S LADY

www.Harlequin.com

Printed in U.S.A.

Other titles by this author
available in ebook format.

FIONA BRAND

lives in the sunny Bay of Islands, New Zealand. Now that both her sons are grown, she continues to love writing books and gardening. After a life-changing time in which she met Christ, she has undertaken study for a bachelor of theology and has become a member of The Order of St. Luke, Christ's healing ministry.

To The Lord, who really did renew my strength while I was writing this book.

"Guard me as the apple of your eye; hide me in the shadow of your wings."

—*Psalm 17*

Acknowledgments:

Huge thanks to Stacy Boyd, my editor,
for her patience, expertise, encouragement and grace.
Thank you!

Prologue

Disbelief and cold fury gripped Branden Tell as he sat in the echoing solitude of a cavernous warehouse. Motes of dust lit by beams of late afternoon sun drifted through the air as he read Jenna Whitmore's latest romantic suspense novel.

The words on the page seemed to swim and shimmer before his eyes. But no matter how hard or how long he looked, the truth he thought had been lost in the smoke and fire and confusion of the past kept stubbornly reforming.

Six ugly letters spelling out *m-u-r-d-e-r*. Black ink on a pulp page: pointing the finger at him.

He broke out in a sweat; his heart was pounding as if he had just run a race. He wondered how much Whitmore actually knew. Given that she had not gone to the police but instead had included the details of his past crime in a novel, he had to assume she probably didn't know much. He was willing to bet she had stumbled on her conclusions by pure, dumb luck.

He blinked rapidly and tried to think. Would anyone else notice the connections Jenna Whitmore had unwittingly made and link them to her cousin's death in a house fire six years ago?

The answer swam up out of the acid burn in his stomach. Marc O'Halloran, the hotshot police detective who had been hunting him with a dogged, relentless focus for the past six years. He would.

Two months ago, almost to the day, O'Halloran had walked into a security firm Branden supplied with alarms while he had been there delivering a consignment. The second he had recognised O'Halloran, he had turned on his heel and left, but he had felt O'Halloran's gaze drilling into his back as he walked.

The close shave had almost given him a heart attack. There was no way O'Halloran could have recognised him, because he had been wearing overalls and a ball cap pulled low over his forehead. He would have looked like a hundred other tradesmen or casual labourers. He had found out later that O'Halloran had been following up on a lead on the fire that had killed his wife and child, checking on who had installed the alarm in his house.

Six years and O'Halloran was still hunting him.

The fear that gripped Branden for long, dizzying moments almost spiralled out of control. He had to think.

No. He had to *do* something.

Snapping the book closed, he found himself staring at the photograph of Jenna Whitmore on the back cover.

She was nothing like her cousin, "The Goddess."

Natalie had been blond, leggy, tanned and gorgeous. Jenna was her polar opposite; dark-haired and pale-skinned with a firm chin and the kind of high, moulded cheekbones that invested her dark eyes with an incisive quality he had always found unsettling.

In that instant, a crude solution formed. After years of wondering when he would appear in one of Jenna's books as a hero, or maybe as some interesting secondary character who could become a hero, he had finally made an appearance, as the villain.

He had mostly read all ten books now, even though he hated reading, because he needed to know if Jenna had written about their shared past. He had found out, just before everything had come to pieces, that Natalie had confided to Jenna that she had a secret friend. For years he had been certain that any evidence that he was linked with Natalie had burned along with everything else in the house, but now he had to assume that Whitmore, who had been close to Natalie, could be sitting on some hard evidence. Since Natalie had been crazy about social networking, it would probably be in the form of emails on Jenna's computer.

His fingers tightened on the novel. In all of the books, the hero had never changed. Whitmore had called him Cutler, Smith, James, Sullivan and a whole host of other names, but the name changes didn't disguise the fact that she was really writing about O'Halloran. The same hard-ass, hero type who had made a habit of ruining Branden's life through the years.

His jaw clenched. O'Halloran had even dated then married The Goddess, the girl *he* should have had.

The distant sound of sirens jerked his head up. For a split second, he thought that it was too late, that the cops were coming for him. He stared a little wildly at the familiar, ordered gloom of the warehouse, and his desk with its neat piles of forms, installation orders and packing notes.

Clamping down on the burst of fear, he strained to listen.

The sirens were receding.

He remembered the fire that, by now, would be a raging inferno. The chemical warehouse would burn for days, soaking up police hours with roadblocks and evacuation procedures. He was safe, for now.

But that didn't change the fact that it was past time he left the country. After the scare two months ago, he had systematically put plans in place: a new identity complete with passport and bank accounts. He had even bought a condo on Australia's Gold Coast. He just needed a little more time to liquidate assets.

He stared at Jenna's face, which, after years of being pretty but slightly plump, had metamorphosed into something approaching beauty. Turning the book over, he studied the cover, his jaw locking. Just to tick him off, the guy they'd put on the cover even looked a little like O'Halloran.

Old rage, fuelled by his intense annoyance that cutting and running was going to cost him big-time, gave birth to a stunning idea. He didn't know why he hadn't thought of it before.

If he was going to lose his business and his expensive, commercial property, which he hadn't been able to offload, damned if he would leave Whitmore and O'Halloran feeling like winners. Instead of venting his temper by flinging the book at a wall of boxes filled with the latest generation of security systems and automated gates, he placed it carefully on his desk, checked his wristwatch and sat down at his computer.

He had almost forgotten that tomorrow was the anniversary of Natalie's death.

Once again it was time to prove that he was a lot more intelligent and creative than anyone had ever given him credit for, past or present.

Including Jenna Whitmore and Marc O'Halloran.

Chapter 1

Pleasurable anticipation hummed through Jenna as she slit open a box stamped with the familiar logo of her publisher. Setting the knife she'd used to cut the packaging tape down on her desk, she extracted a glossy, trade-sized paperback: her latest novel. Glancing at the back cover copy, she flipped the book over to check out the cover...and for long seconds her mind went utterly blank.

Swamping shadows flowed over broad, sleek shoulders and a lean, muscled torso. Moonlight glimmered across sculpted cheekbones, a blade-straight nose and a rock-solid jaw. By some trick of the light, for a heart-pounding moment, the dark, molten gaze of the man depicted on the cover, shaded by inky lashes, appeared to stare directly into hers.

Her breath hitched in her throat as her sunny office

faded and she was spun back nine years, to the stifling heat of a darkened, moonlight-dappled apartment, Marc O'Halloran and a fatal attraction she thought she had controlled.

Memories flooded back, some bittersweet, others hot and edged and earthy. The clean scent of his skin as he had shrugged out of his shirt, the sensual shock of his kiss. Heart-stopping moments later, the weight of his body pressing down on hers...

Groping blindly for her chair, Jenna sat down. Her heart was hammering and her legs felt as limp as noodles, which was crazy. After nine years, the few weeks during which she had dated O'Halloran—and the one out-of-control night after they had broken up when she had made love with him—shouldn't have still registered. Especially since she had spent more time avoiding him than she had ever spent mooning over him.

More to the point, she had gotten over him. It had taken time, the process had been a lot more difficult than she had expected, but she had moved on with her life.

Taking a steadying breath, she forced herself to dispassionately study the masculine image that decorated the front cover of the novel.

It wasn't O'Halloran. Plain common sense dictated that fact. Like her, O'Halloran lived in Auckland, and the book had been published and printed in New York. The cover model would have been someone picked from an agency list in Manhattan.

By some freak chance, whoever had designed the cover had just somehow managed to choose a model who looked like O'Halloran.

At a second glance, the differences were clear. The

model's nose was thinner, longer, and his mouth was fuller. As broodingly handsome as he was, overall he was just a little too perfect. He lacked the masculine toughness to his features that was a defining characteristic of O'Halloran, the remote quality to his gaze that spelled out that O'Halloran was neither gym-pumped nor cosmetically enhanced. He was that breed apart: a cop.

Frowning, she replaced the book back in the open carton, closed the flaps and stowed the box under the desk, out of sight.

Feeling distinctly unsettled, she strolled out to the kitchen and made herself a cup of tea, using the calming routine of selecting a fragrant fruit variety and a pretty mug to put herself back into work mode. The distant sound of a siren almost made her spill hot tea over her fingers and shoved another memory back at her.

The last time she had seen O'Halloran had been from a distance, four years ago, when she had narrowly avoided running into him in town. Dressed in a suit and wearing a shoulder holster, he had been on police business. The grim remoteness of his expression and the presence of the weapon had underlined the reason she couldn't afford him in her life. Maybe her reaction had been a little over-the-top, but after losing both her father and her fiancé to military front lines, the last thing she had needed was to fall for a police detective. Like soldiers, cops bled. More to the point, in the line of duty, they died.

She had seen what being married to a soldier had done to her mother; the separations and the constant fear, the shock when the bad news finally came followed by intense, bone-deep grief.

Less than a year later, her mother had died of cancer. Jenna had read the specialists' reports and listened to the medical experts but that hadn't shifted her inner certainty that what her mother had really died of had been a broken heart.

The final kicker had been when, even knowing the risk, straight out of high school she had gotten engaged to a soldier. Dane had also been her best friend, which was probably why he had slipped beneath her defences. But that hadn't changed the fact that he had died in a hot, sun-blasted foreign country on some covert mission.

A week after it had happened she had finally been informed. In the midst of her grief, somehow the fact that Dane had been lying cold and dead in a hospital morgue for seven days, while she had spent that time shopping and planning for a wedding, had added to her disorientation. She had loved Dane. She should have known something was wrong. Instead, she had been choosing invitations and having fittings for a dress she would never wear. Her own lack of connection to a man she had been prepared to marry had been subtly shocking. It had underlined a distance, a separation, from Dane that she had witnessed in her parents' marriage, and in that moment she had understood something basic about herself. She couldn't live that life.

She needed to be loved. And not only loved, but also to be the cherished focus of the man she chose.

Fingers shaking slightly, a ridiculous overreaction, she placed the mug on a coaster and seated herself in front of her computer.

Maybe her need for a deep, committed love was unrealistic and overly romantic, but she knew her nature.

As much as she had wanted to share her life with Dane, she knew now that it would never have worked. She couldn't compete with the adrenaline and danger of combat and undercover missions.

She couldn't afford to fall for anyone who was going to place themselves on the front lines, either militarily or as a civilian.

She refreshed the screen and found herself staring at a manuscript page from the book she was currently editing. A love scene.

Jamming the lid of the laptop down, she strode out of her office and grabbed a jacket. She needed air, lots of it. Stepping out onto her porch, she closed the front door of her house and locked it behind her.

But slamming the lid on the Pandora's Box of her past was more difficult. As she walked, more memories flickered in a series of freeze frames. The undertow of fascination she had felt the first time she had seen O'Halloran. The bone-melting excitement of their first kiss, as his big hand had curled around her nape and his mouth had settled on hers.

Her stomach clenched. Emotions and sensations she had thought long dead flared to life. She felt like a sleeper waking up, her pulse too fast, her skin ultra-sensitive; she could smell more, hear more, feel more. It had been years since she had felt so alive and, with a jolt, she realised that it had been years since she had felt anything much at all.

As a professional writer, her life was necessarily ordered and quiet. She worked long hours to meet her deadlines, and most evenings she went online to chat with fans or reply to emails. A couple of times a year she travelled to conferences and did promotional tours, coinciding with the release of her books. Apart from socialising for business, *cloistered* was the term that came to mind.

At the age of twenty-nine, thanks to her solitary career, and the pressure of work created by the success of her books, she had a gap the size of a yawning abyss in her social and sexual life.

Thanks to an inconvenient perfectionist streak that had seemed to become more pronounced with every year, she had trouble meeting anyone with whom she could visualise having an intimate, meaningful relationship.

As in sex.

Another hot flashback to the night in O'Halloran's apartment made her stomach clench and her breasts tighten. She definitely wasn't a nun, but for nine years she had lived like one. She hadn't set out to be so isolated and alone—lacking almost any semblance of human warmth in her life, lacking the mate she wanted—it was just the way things had worked out.

Or was it?

The feeling of constriction in her chest increased as she examined the extremity of her reaction to the cover of her new book.

She had gotten over the loss of both of her parents; and she had gotten over Dane. The fact that they had never slept together, because he had surprised her by proposing literally minutes before he had shipped out, had meant they had never had the chance at a full, intimate relationship. As much as she'd loved him, in her mind, he would forever remain a part of her childhood and teen years, not a part of her adult life.

For the past few years, as much as she had wanted to

find someone she could fall for, marry and have babies with, she hadn't come even remotely close.

As outwardly attractive as her dates had been, there had always been something wrong. They had been either too short, or too tall, or their personalities just hadn't appealed. She had been picky to the point that most of her friends had long since given up introducing her to eligible bachelors.

Now she had to consider that the reason she had never been able to move on to the healthy, normal relationship she craved was because at some deep, instinctual level, O'Halloran still mattered. That in the weeks they had dated—and maybe because he was the first and only man she had ever made love with—in a primitive, purely masculine way, he had somehow managed to imprint himself on her so deeply that she had never been able to open up to another relationship.

She stopped dead, barely noticing the trees that dappled the sidewalk with chilly shade, or the young mother with a stroller who walked past her. It was even possible that in some sneaky, undermining way, she had fallen for O'Halloran because of his dangerous occupation; that the reason she wasn't attracted to a "normal" nine-to-five guy was because her years on military bases had hardwired her to be attracted to edgy alpha types.

She forced herself back into motion again, automatically turning down the street that led to a small park. The sick feeling in her stomach increased as she strolled, along with the desire to bang her head against the nearest wall she could find in the hope that that salutary action might jolt some sense into her.

She felt like she was staring down a long tunnel inscribed with the words *obvious reason for multiple re-lationship failures*.

Now was not a good time to realise that as hard as she'd tried to bury her past and the attraction to O'Halloran, like the heroine in her book, she hadn't succeeded.

And now it had come back to bite her.

Two hours before midnight, and the clock was ticking....

On edge and gripped by a tense air of expectation, *haunted by a past that had teeth*, Marc O'Halloran, clad in a pair of grey interlock track pants that hung low on his hips, closed the door on his private gym. A towel from the shower he'd just taken slung over one muscled shoulder, he padded through the darkened luxury of his Auckland waterfront apartment, not bothering to turn on lights.

Stepping out on his terrace, he allowed the damp chill to settle around him like a shroud as he stared broodingly out at the spectacular view of the Waitemata Harbour. To one side, the graceful arch of the Harbour Bridge was almost obscured by a wraithlike veil of mist, and the headland that was Devonport, with its naval base and steep streets crammed with houses, glittered quietly.

Below, street-lighting from the busy viaduct glowed through the wrought-iron railing that edged his terrace. The pulse of neon lighting from the busy restaurants and bars flickered garishly in time with the beat of a jazz band, adding a strident, unsettling rhythm to the night.

As Marc stepped back into his lounge, the glass of

the bi-fold doors threw his reflection back at him. The scars that marred his right shoulder and his forearms were an unwelcome reminder of the house fire that had taken the lives of his wife and small son six years ago. Luckily, the broken neck, courtesy of the falling beam that had also damaged his shoulder, hadn't required surgery or scars, just months in a neck brace.

Nothing too major, he thought grimly. He had lived.

Walking through to the laundry, he tossed the towel in a basket, grabbed a fresh T-shirt out of the dryer and pulled it on. Minutes later, after collecting a glass of ice water from the kitchen, he entered his study. The view of the port, and the shimmer of city lights, winked out as he switched on a lamp and unlocked his briefcase.

Bypassing the correspondence file from the security business in which he was a partner, he searched out the bookstore bag that contained the novel he had bought during his lunch break.

Hot off the presses, the latest Jenna Whitmore.

With an effort of will, he shook off the miasma of guilt that went with the impending anniversary of his wife's and child's deaths, and the hot burn of frustration that the only crime he had never been able to solve had been the murder of his own family. Dropping the paper bag on the gleaming surface of his desk, he studied the cover with its tense, dark backdrop.

The book was a suspense, but also a romance, not something he normally read, but he had once dated Jenna so, out of curiosity, he had bought her first book.

To his surprise he had been hooked from the first page. Despite her link to his past—one of the links that he had systematically eradicated from his life—Jenna's books had become a guilty pleasure and a deep, dark secret. If the detectives he had used to work with at Auckland Central or his business partner in the security business he now part-owned, Ben McCabe, ever found out that he read romances, he would never live it down.

Automatically, he turned the book over and examined the publicity photo on the back cover. Despite the tension that coursed through him, he found himself gradually relaxing. Jenna, who also happened to be his dead wife's cousin, frequently changed her hair. The constant process of reinvention never failed to fascinate Marc.

This time she had opted for caramel streaks to complement her natural dark colour and a long, layered cut. As modern as the cut was, the overall effect was oddly elegant.

When they had dated, even though it had only been for a short time, he had liked Jenna's hair exactly how it had been, long and soft and completely natural. Although he was willing to be converted by the lighter streaks and the sexy cut, which highlighted the delicate curve of her cheekbones and made her dark eyes look long and unexpectedly smoky.

Settling into a black leather armchair set to one side of the desk, he propped his bare feet on an ottoman and flipped open the book.

The vice-like grip of guilt and frustration, the knowledge that approximately an hour from now, the man who had murdered his family would contact him, slowly eased as he forced himself to turn pages.

Reluctantly engrossed by words that flowed with a neat, no-nonsense economy, Marc ceased to notice the silence of his Auckland apartment and the inner tension that sawed at his nerves.

As the minutes flowed past, he sank deeper into the story, noting that it was her best yet. The hero, Cutler, a detective, had a lot of grit and texture, and the procedural details were right on the button.

The plot reached a crescendo as Cutler and the heroine, Sara, after a series of tantalising near misses, finally, electrifyingly, made it to Cutler's apartment.

Unexpected tension burned through Marc as he was drawn through the passionate interlude. By the time he had reached the end of the love scene, he had ceased to visualise the damp chill of a rainy afternoon, and instead his mind had shifted to another season, another room, filled with heated shadows and moonlight....

The sound of distant sirens brought his head up, an automatic reaction that, after two years out of the force, he hadn't been able to kick.

His jaw tightened. Thinking about Jenna was crazy. Since his wife, Natalie, and their baby had died in a house fire, Marc had had no interest in another committed relationship. He had enough guilt to process.

Added to that, he hadn't seen Jenna in years and, apart from one unplanned episode *after* they had broken up and following a near accident with a car, they had never made it anywhere near a bedroom.

A vivid memory of Jenna scrambling off the couch they'd ended up sprawled across nine years ago, moonlight flowing over the pale curves of her body, jolted him out of the story altogether. A new tension coursing through him, he put the book down.

Broodingly, he recalled flickering images of her fastening the low back of her dress. The tense expression on her face as she'd searched for shoes and her handbag. She had refused a lift and waved her cell at him, indicating she had already called a cab.

Marc hadn't pushed it. The fact that they had slept together after they had broken up had underpinned the awkward minutes until the cab she'd ordered had slid into his drive.

The blinding fact that it had been Jenna's first time had added to the tension, although Jenna had brushed it off. He could still remember her quiet assertion that if it hadn't been for the adrenaline-charged moments when Marc had stepped in and saved her from being hit by an obviously drunk driver, what had just taken place on his couch would never have happened.

Marc had had to accept her self-contained approach. He'd been aware that she hadn't liked the fact that he was a police detective or that he commanded an armed first response team, the Special Tactics Squad.

When he'd started dating Jenna's cousin, Natalie had held a similar view. She hadn't liked the long work hours, the seaminess or the danger, and she hadn't liked being closed out of that part of his life.

After the first year of marriage, Natalie had wanted him to quit the force and go back to law, in which he had a degree. His parents, both lawyers, had their own successful law firm, and she hadn't been able to understand why he didn't want to be a part of it.

The argument had been the start of a wedge in their relationship he hadn't been able to mend. When it came down to it he preferred the practical, hands-on approach to justice that police work offered him, rather than the intricacies of negotiating the legal system.

The whoosh of incoming mail on his computer brought his head up. Tension slammed into Marc as he noted the time: eleven o'clock, exactly. He had been so engrossed by the book, and the window into the past it had opened, that he had forgotten the time.

Jaw taut, he strolled to his desk and read the email.

The message was simple. The same message he had received every year for the past five years on the anniversary of the house fire. A fire he had been certain had been started deliberately, an act of revenge by the notorious criminal family he had been investigating at the time.

Catch me if you can.

Cold anger edged with frustration burned through Marc. Although, there was a certain relief in the fact that the waiting was over. Punching the print button, he waited for the hard copy of the taunting message to feed out.

He had never been able to trace the message to an actual person, or prove the message was connected to the crime. Each time he had traced the email to the server, the name and physical address hadn't panned out. The trail had been predictable, a string of stolen identities, mostly deceased persons, through which cash payments via fake bank accounts had been made. Non-existent people and random addresses, all added up to a wild-goose chase.

Despite his contention that the house fire that had killed his family and put him in hospital had been a copycat crime committed by someone other than the serial arsonist the police had been hunting at the time, no one had bought into his theory. Since the arsonist had died during a shootout just after he had tried to set a police station on fire, there was no one to question. The supposed perpetrator was dead, the fires had stopped, end of story.

Grimly, Marc filed the message with the others in a heavy manila folder that contained every police or fire department report and newspaper article relating to the fire and the death of his wife and small son.

Maybe he was being obsessive about his hunt for a shadowy criminal. Maybe he had been wrong all along, and the investigative team who had sifted through what was left of his house were right. The psychological reports that had finished his police career were adamant on that point.

Even so, Marc couldn't let go. The two people he had cared about most had died of smoke inhalation when he should have been at home, protecting them. Instead, he had used his free time—the quality time he should have been spending with his family—working surveillance on a powerful criminal family who had slipped the net on his last operation.

Courtesy of the injuries he had sustained getting Natalie and tiny Jared out of the house, he had ended up flat on his back in hospital for weeks. Further months on sick leave while he had waited for his neck and shoulder to heal, followed by reconstructive surgery for his shoulder, had added to his frustration. By the time he had been fit for duty again, the case had been closed.

He was no longer a detective, but he had not dropped the case. Thanks to bequests from his grandparents and a talent for investment, Marc was independently wealthy. Enough so that he had been able to buy in to the security business he presently co-owned and could afford to fund an ongoing private investigation into the case.

When he had finally woken up from sedation in hospital to find that both Natalie and Jared had died, grief and cold fury hit him like a blow. Despite the gloomy prognosis on his fractured neck, he had made a vow.

It was too late to save his family, but he would use his talent for solving crime, which had resulted in their deaths, to bring the man he was certain had murdered them to justice.

He hadn't made a significant breakthrough in the six years he had chased leads and walked down investigative dead alleys. But the murderer who was taunting him would make a mistake, and when he did Marc would be waiting.

It was just a matter of time.

Chapter 2

An hour before midnight, *and the anniversary of Natalie's death*.

Jenna walked through the darkened parking lot of the shopping mall in central Auckland, glad for the casual warmth of jeans and boots and the cashmere coat belted around her waist to push back the chill.

Overhead, thick clouds hid any hint of moon or stars. On the ground, streamers of cold mist rose off damp concrete and wreathed ranks of wet, glistening cars, adding a dismal air to a chilly winter's night.

Behind her, footsteps echoed, the tread uncannily mirroring her own so that at first she had thought the step was just an echo.

Adjusting her grip on the carrier bags, which thumped against her legs with every step, she walked a little faster, although speeding up was an effort. She was tired from a string of late nights and too many hours spent at her computer. From the scratchiness at the back of her throat and the sensitivity of her eyes, she suspected she was also coming down with a virus. The diagnosis was further confirmed by the chills that periodically swept her and the aches and pains that seemed to have sunk into her bones.

She strained to listen behind her and logged the moment the change in her pace put whoever was following her out of sync with her step.

Automatically, her too-fertile writer's brain analysed the tread. There was no sharp tap of heels. The sound was more deliberate, solid, so it was likely the person wasn't female. He was probably one of the young guys she had seen hanging at the entrance to the mall on her way out.

Now that she knew there was definitely someone behind her, the fact that he hadn't either veered off, or walked briskly past, but had chosen to remain approximately the same distance behind and maintain her snail's pace sent a chill shooting down her spine. The farther she walked away from the lights of the mall, the more sinister the trailing footsteps had become.

As she approached an SUV, in an effort to catch a glimpse of whoever was behind her, she slowed and glanced in the wing mirror.

Apart from wet cars and dark, thin air wreathed with mist, as far back as she could see, the parking lot appeared to be empty.

In that same instant, she registered that the footsteps had stopped. Somehow that was more frightening than if she had actually caught a glimpse of whoever had been following her.

Heart pounding, she swung around and skimmed the rows of cars. The background hum of city traffic, the distant blare of a car horn, seemed to increase the sense of isolation in the misty parking lot, the muffling, encapsulating silence.

Somewhere off to the left a car engine coughed to life. She let out a relieved breath. Mystery solved. Whoever had been behind her must have stopped to unlock their car just seconds before she had gotten up the courage to check on him.

Castigating herself for the paranoia that had leaped at her from nowhere, she adjusted her grip on the carrier bags, and continued on toward her car.

She had parked on the far side of the lot, next to the clothing department stores, because when she'd made the decision to do some late night shopping, she hadn't originally counted on buying groceries. Her goal had simply been to get out of her house, away from her office and the memories that, at this time of year, always seemed to press in on her.

Normally a dedicated shopper, happy to price and compare until she found exactly what she wanted, she'd found the items she'd needed too quickly. Unwilling to leave the bright cheerfulness of the mall and the simple human comfort of being amongst people, even if no one bothered to speak to her unless she handed money over a counter, she'd strolled on into the supermarket.

Shopping this late was ridiculous; the task could have waited until morning. But tomorrow was the anniversary of her cousin Natalie's death and she hadn't wanted to do anything as frivolous as buy pretty clothes. Especially since her aunt and uncle, who still struggled with their grief, expected her over for dinner.

Behind her, she could hear the car her "stalker" had climbed into accelerating toward the exit, going too fast. She caught a glimpse of a glossy, black sedan, pumped up at the back, and the flare of taillights as he braked. It occurred to her that the car, an Audi, looked like the same model the villain had used in her latest book, which seemed appropriate.

Annoyance at the casual cruelty of the man, if he really had been trying to scare her, replaced the last wimpy remnants of fear. She didn't normally wish bad things on people, but a sudden, vivid fantasy of the Audi being pulled over and the driver being issued with an offence notice was warming.

Feeling a whole lot more cheerful, she angled across the lot toward her car.

Ahead, a noisy group of young people exited the mall and stopped right next to the shiny new Porsche she had bought to celebrate the release of her book. She saw with relief that they were trailed by a uniformed mall security guard who was keeping an eye on them.

Simultaneously she registered that the obnoxious Audi, which had apparently missed the exit ramp, was now doing another circuit of the lot. Distracted by the kids milling around her car, she sped up. As she did so, she automatically hitched the carrier bags higher and in that instant one of the handles broke and the contents of the bag cascaded onto the pavement.

Staggering a little at the sudden release of weight on one side and muttering beneath her breath, Jenna set the bags down. Luckily the bag that had broken had been filled with packets and cans, not fruits and vegetables. One eye on the kids, who were still grouped around her

Porsche, she started retrieving cans, some of which had skittered across the lane.

As she bent to pick up a packet of rice, the throaty sound of an engine caused her to jerk her head up. Twin headlights pinned her. Adrenaline shoved through her veins, momentarily freezing her in place. The black car, which she had momentarily forgotten, was roaring straight for her.

Dropping the rice and cans, she flung herself into a gap between two cars, hitting the wet concrete of the parking lot a split second before the car accelerated past, so close the vibration shimmered up through pavement and hot exhaust filled her nostrils.

Loose hair tangled around her face, Jenna pushed into a sitting position, logging grazed palms that burned, and a knee that seemed temporarily frozen and which would hurt like blazes in a minute or two. Thankfully, her handbag, which had been slung over one shoulder, was on the ground next to her, although the contents, including her car keys and phone, had spilled across the concrete.

"Are you all right?"

The calm male voice jerked her head up. For a split second, heart still pounding with an overload of adrenaline, she saw O'Halloran. The illusion winked out almost immediately since, apart from hair color and a lean, muscular build, the security officer didn't look anything like her long-ago ex.

Although, she could be forgiven the error, she thought a little grimly, as she allowed him to help her to her feet.

The last time she'd had a run-in with a car, nine

years ago to be exact, it *had* been O'Halloran who had come to her rescue.

She noted the name on a badge pinned to the pocket of the security officer's shirt and dredged up a thin smile for Mathews. "I'm fine, thank you. Just a few bruises."

And a whole lot of mangled shopping.

While Mathews asked her questions about the near miss and made some notes, Jenna tested out her knee. It hurt and was already stiffening, but at least she could put weight on it. Although, it would be black and blue by morning.

Limping, she began gathering up her things, starting with the contents of her handbag. The rice was history, grains were scattered all over the concrete, but she found the broken plastic bag and stuffed it into another carrier bag, along with other grocery items that had rolled loose.

Mathews collected the bags containing her dress and shoes and insisted on carrying everything to her car and stowing them for her.

As he closed the passenger side door he cast a steely look at the kids, who had drifted farther down the mall and were now grouped outside a café.

"Are you sure you're okay? If you need medical attention we've got a first-aid station in the mall."

Ignoring the burning pain from the scrapes on her palms, Jenna checked in her handbag, found a business card and handed it to him. "I'm okay. The only thing I'd like is the registration of the vehicle, if you can get it."

He tucked her card in his shirt pocket. "No problem. I'll check out the security footage, but with the lights at this end of the lot knocked out by vandals and the mist, I can't guarantee anything."

Feeling increasingly stiff and sore, Jenna climbed into the leather-scented interior of the Porsche although, for once, she couldn't take pleasure in the car. With a convulsive movement, she locked the doors, fastened her seat belt then sat staring at her shaking hands and grazed palms.

No, she definitely wasn't *okay*.

The driver of the black Audi had to have seen her. She had been standing in the middle of the lane, caught in the glare of his headlights, and yet he hadn't so much as slowed down. If she hadn't gotten out of his way she would have been hit. At the speed he had been travelling, she would have been, at the very least, seriously injured.

Maybe she was going crazy, or she'd written one too many suspense stories, but she was almost certain that what had happened hadn't been either a joke or an accident.

Someone had just tried to kill her.

Lamplight pooled around Jenna as, too wired to sleep after the near miss in the mall parking lot, she set a mug of hot chocolate down on her desk and booted up her computer. Sliding her glasses onto the bridge of her nose, she vetoed any idea that she could work on her manuscript. Since she couldn't settle to sleep, it stood to reason that she was way too jittery to write.

Clicking on the mail icon, she decided to stick with the less brain-intensive task of answering emails until she got tired enough to actually sleep. Her laptop beeped as a small flood of emails filled her inbox.

Minutes later, she opened an email and froze. Fighting a cold sense of disorientation, she pushed her glasses a little higher on her nose and forced herself to reread the message that had just appeared in her fan mail account.

I hate your latest book in which you have portrayed ME as the villin. Besides the romance and the hero being unreel (no one looks that good) the villin is not as bad as you're making out, he deserves a medal for not trying to do away with Sara in the first chapter. Take "Deadly Valentine" off the market NOW. If you don't you will regret it.

Jenna drew a long, impeded breath. As chilling as the content was, and the veiled threat, the writer of the email, ekf235, had no particular literary aspirations. He had misspelt *villain* and *unreal* and had committed the cardinal sin of joining two independent clauses with a comma instead of a semicolon. If her editor, Rachel, saw it, she would have a fit.

Jenna sat back in her office chair, her normal determination to see the positive side of every fan letter she received, even if it was scathingly critical, absent. The misspellings and dreadful grammar, the sideswipe about her characterisation, didn't take away from the fact that whoever had written the letter was nutty enough to think she had patterned the villain on him.

Since Jenna had never heard of ekf235, let alone corresponded with him, that claim was highly unlikely.

For long seconds, Jenna stared at the screen of her laptop, and tried to catalogue all of the men she had known through her life, but her mind seemed to have frozen. It was mild shock, she realized.

For the second time in one night.

Hooking her glasses off the bridge of her nose, she sat back in her chair, and rubbed at the sharp little throb that had developed at her temples.

She was tired and sore, despite taking a couple of painkillers and rubbing arnica and liniment into her bruised knee. She shouldn't have started on emails this late. Buying in to the ramblings of an emotionally disturbed person, who didn't have the courage to reveal their real identity, was always a mistake.

Taking another deep breath, she let it out slowly and tapped the button that generated her auto-reply, thanking the fan. A small whooshing sound indicated that the reply had gone.

She glanced at her collage board, which was littered with all of the various materials she had used as inspiration for the highly successful series of novels that had shot her to the top of bestseller lists.

The only photos she had were those of various male and female models, which she'd cut out of magazines over the years to provide inspiration for her heroes and heroines.

Massaging the throb in her temple with fingers that still shook annoyingly, she wondered what O'Halloran would think about the cowardly, threatening email then pulled herself up short. After the episode with her new book cover, then the moment in the mall parking lot, she had decided that for her own emotional well-being, the sooner she managed to cut O'Halloran out of her life, past and present, the better.

Blinking away tiredness, she examined the rest of the board, which was littered with snapshots and pictures of houses, landscape settings and assorted weaponry.

She had not amassed anything much about a villain. As a rule of thumb, she had found that the less that was said about a villain the better. Mystery was far scarier than knowledge and, besides, fans of her stories responded to the hero, not the bad guy.

Picking up her hot chocolate, she sipped and let her mind go loose, a technique she used to help with memory, especially for allowing seemingly insignificant details to surface. She frowned when her mind remained a stubborn blank.

The person who had emailed had claimed that she had used him as the villain, which meant she must have met him at some stage. There was always the danger that, subliminally, she could have remembered and applied characteristics from someone she had known in her past. In *Deadly Valentine*, she had been influenced by a couple of incidents from the past, but she was also aware that those incidents—the delivery of a single rose and a secret online "lover"—were neither new nor unusual elements.

One thing was sure, no one she had ever met, or knew, came even close to the devious fictional criminal who had hunted Sara down in *Deadly Valentine*.

The only character she had ruthlessly drawn from real life was the heroine, Sara, a private investigator whom Jenna had based on herself. Somehow her own persona and single lifestyle had seemed to fit Sara Chisolm even better than they fitted Jenna.

In the fictional world Sara moved in, living alone was a bonus. Although maybe the fact that Sara was a little on the hard-boiled side and far more confident in the bedroom than Jenna could ever pretend to be had something to do with that.

Her finger hovered over the delete button, but in a moment of caution, she decided she couldn't afford to blot the email out of existence altogether. The meticulous filing habit she had nurtured over the past eight years of researching detective and police procedural material for her books was too ingrained. In eight years she had not deleted one piece of correspondence without first obtaining a hard copy, and she was not starting now.

She didn't expect to hear back from the poisonous fan. Her innocuous thank-you email was designed to neutralise unpleasantness, and it usually worked, but that didn't mean she shouldn't be cautious.

She pressed the print button and waited for the sheet to feed out.

The internet provided a forum for a lot of flaky people. Most of them were harmless. The thought that the vague threat in the email could eventuate into an actual problem was something she was determined she was not going to lose any sleep over, but she couldn't dismiss it altogether.

As a writer, she had lost count of the number of times an inconsequential document had proved pivotal in her fictional investigations. Perhaps that was why the email had felt so chilling.

Shoving the hard copy into the plain folder that contained her negative fan mail, and which she kept in the bottom drawer of her desk, she deleted the email.

On impulse, to balance out the unpleasantness, Jenna opened a folder in which she kept all of the mail she received from the technical experts who helped her with research. She selected the file containing all of the correspondence from Lydell88.

As she read through the last couple of emails, the tension that had gripped her faded. Lydell wasn't exactly a shoulder to cry on, but reading his no-nonsense prose was, in an odd way, steadying.

There was nothing to indicate where Lydell88 lived. All she knew was that he was an Auckland cop with considerable experience, and that he didn't mind answering her occasional questions. She had found him by emailing the Auckland District Office. One of the detectives had eventually responded by supplying her with Lydell88's email address.

Generally he supplied precise police procedural information, but over the years he had begun making incisive, relevant comments about her plots and characterisation, indicating that at some point, he had begun to read her books.

His compliments were sparing, but she valued them all the more for that. When he liked something, he was unequivocal about the matter and she basked in the glow for days.

Lately, he had even begun to suggest plot lines she could develop in future books. The ideas were well thought out and stemmed from an intimate knowledge of her characters and an even better understanding of the criminal mind.

However, she was aware that wasn't what gave her the warm glow of delight every time she opened one of his emails.

Over the years, talking with Lydell88 about the technicalities of developing the police procedural side to her stories had, in an odd way, become the closest thing she had gotten to a date that she could actually enjoy, which was strange considering that he was a cop.

She guessed it came down to mutual interests. They both enjoyed the books, she as the writer, he as a reader and researcher. Somehow, those two things had gelled along with a subtle, intangible quality she could only call chemistry, and they had become immersed, together, in that fictional world.

When her editor had holidayed with her last summer, Jenna had allowed her limited access to the file, keeping the more private exchanges to herself. It had seemed too personal to share the conversations they'd had about the romance of the postwar era, or that Lydell88 thought she should try her hand at writing in that period.

Rachel had been riveted, and they had spent the long summer evenings trying to profile Lydell88. And, more importantly, trying to decide what he looked like.

Jenna hadn't received anything from Lydell88 lately. He generally only ever instigated discussions about her latest book, a line in the sand of which she was sharply aware. Early on, she had considered the fact that he could be either elderly or married, but had rejected both ideas. The tone and style of Lydell88's emails suggested he was younger rather than older, and at no time during their discussions had he ever mentioned a partner, or children, so she assumed he was single.

Respecting his desire for privacy, and relieved that there was no pressure for their discussions to be anything more than they were, she limited her contacts by only initiating correspondence when she started a new book and needed to check facts.

She was waiting with anticipation to see what he thought of *Deadly Valentine*, although it was early days since it had only just been released into stores.

Closing down the program and the laptop, she

hooked her glasses off the bridge of her nose and set them beside the keyboard. The pleasant glow she had received from rereading Lydell88's last email faded as she noticed her bottom drawer, which contained her negative fan mail, wasn't quite closed.

Nudging the drawer shut with her foot, she collected her empty mug and switched out the lights, but the damage was done. As hard as she tried to dismiss it, the unpleasant threat delivered by ekf235 had rocked her.

Feeling abruptly exhausted, Jenna stepped into her warmly lit hallway and closed her study door. Limping through to the kitchen, she rinsed the mug and placed it in the dishwasher then began her nightly routine of checking locks.

She had bought the roomy old Victorian house a couple of years ago with the royalties from her first six books, and as wonderful as it was, it had a lot of doors. Despite her attempt to remain upbeat, the silence seemed to ring as she walked through the house. For the first time, instead of taking pleasure in the elegant ranks of French doors and tall sash windows, she couldn't help noticing the large amount of glass through which she could, conceivably, be watched.

Despite the luxurious kilim rugs she had strewn on the glossy, kauri wood floors, her footsteps echoed eerily. As she switched out lamps, shadows seemed to flood the large, rambling rooms, sending a preternatural chill down her spine and making her vividly aware that she was very much alone.

Security wasn't an issue, she reminded herself. The property was alarmed and gated and her fence was high and in good repair. A brief glance at the blinking light of the alarm system she'd had installed shortly after she had moved in assured her that the house was secure.

Jenna carried a glass of water up the long, sweeping staircase lined with, admittedly, gloomy Whitmore family portraits. She avoided the dark stares of ranks of long-dead relatives. Lately the sepia-toned record of the past and her lack of current family portraits had become a depressing reminder of the emptiness of her personal life.

It was one o'clock before she finally climbed into the elegant French provincial-style bed she had bought in response to an article she'd read on curing insomnia.

Apparently, there were two keys to getting a good night's sleep: forming a routine and setting the scene for a restful night.

She was hopeless at the first, so she'd decided she could at least make her bedroom look as serene and inviting as impossible. With dark teak wood and white-on-white bed linen and furnishings, her bedroom could have been lifted straight out of a movie set. Unfortunately, that fact didn't seem to make any difference to her sleep pattern, which was erratic.

As she switched off the light she became aware of sirens somewhere in the distance and recalled the current story in the news. Apparently there was a serial arsonist on the loose, a creepy coincidence since six years ago a serial arsonist had been responsible for Natalie's and her baby's deaths.

She stared at a bright sliver of moonlight beaming through a gap in the heavy cream drapes and found herself fixated on the possible identity of her poisonous fan.

She had not been callous enough to use Natalie's mysterious death in her story, but she *had* drawn on the fact that Natalie had had a secret online friend who had sent her Valentine's-style gifts: single long-stemmed white roses and chocolates.

Although the idea that the person who had sent the threatening email could be Natalie's long-ago secret admirer was definitely pushing theory into the realms of fantasy.

It had to be a coincidence that she had received the email on the anniversary of Natalie's death.

Chapter 3

The next afternoon, Jenna drove to the cemetery. The cars occupying almost every space and the large numbers of well-dressed people walking through the grounds signalled that a funeral was in progress.

Gathering the bunch of flowers she had placed on the backseat, she slipped dark glasses on the bridge of her nose and strolled through the grounds. The sun was warm, the air crisp, the sky a clear, dazzling blue. Large oaks cast cooling shade on row after row of well-tended plots.

As she neared the vicinity of Natalie's grave, she noted the lone figure of a man. For a split second she thought it could be O'Halloran. Her heart slammed against her chest then she dismissed the idea. The man was tall, but not tall enough, and on the lean side rather than muscular. He was also wearing a ball cap, something that she had never seen O'Halloran wear.

A large group of mourners moving toward the parking lot obscured her view. The next time Jenna got a clear view of the gravesite, that part of the cemetery was deserted.

She strolled the rest of the distance to the grave, which was already decorated with a wreath of pink roses and a tiny blue teddy bear, which Aunt Mary would have placed there first thing that morning. Blinking back the automatic rush of tears at her aunt and uncle's pain, which, after all the years, showed no sign of abating, she unwrapped the bunch of bright yellow and pink chrysanthemums she'd bought from the local florist, and placed them in a stone vase set to one side of the headstone.

Extracting a bottle of water from her purse, she topped up the vase. Straightening, she stepped back to admire her handiwork, and became aware that she was no longer alone. She spun a little too quickly, wincing as her knee, still stiff and sore, twinged. The plastic bottle bounced on the grass as a large hand briefly cupped her elbow.

A small shock ran through her as she processed dark, cool eyes beneath black brows, clean-cut cheekbones and a tough jaw made even edgier by a five o'clock shadow.

For a split second, even though she knew it was O'Halloran, she had trouble accepting that fact. Six years had passed since she had last seen him up close, and in that time he had changed. His hair was still the same, dark and close-cut, his skin olive and tanned, but his face was leaner than she remembered, his gaze more remote. A scar decorated the bridge of his nose, and his chest and shoulders were broader, as if he worked out regularly, which, given the rehab he'd had to do following his operation, was probably the case.

The rough jaw, oddly in keeping with his long-sleeved T-shirt and black pants, added a wolfish quality that signalled that whatever else O'Halloran had been doing, he hadn't taken the time to shave. A small quiver shot down her spine when she realized that O'Halloran was studying her just as intently as she was studying him, and suddenly, the notion that the large, fierce male looming over her had anything remotely in common with the model who had posed for the cover of her latest book was ludicrous. "I didn't expect to find you here."

Instantly, Jenna regretted the bluntness of the comment, even though it was true. Since Natalie's and Jared's deaths, O'Halloran had almost completely distanced himself from the family, politely declining all invitations. According to her aunt and uncle he seemed to have no interest in visiting the grave. She had certainly never seen him here any other time she had visited, or seen any evidence that he left flowers.

O'Halloran retrieved the empty water bottle and handed it to her. "I visit. I just try to keep out of Mary's way. The stuffed toys are hard to take."

The blankness of O'Halloran's gaze made her chest squeeze tight. For the first time, she saw it for what it was, grasped just how deeply O'Halloran had been affected by the loss of his family. It was etched in his face, in the muscle pulsing along the side of his jaw.

He had not attended the funeral because he had been flat on his back in hospital at the time.

While he was injured, she had worried about him to

the point that she had tried ringing him and, once, had even gone looking for him. She hadn't found him. Like a wounded animal, O'Halloran had gone to ground. Months later, he had surfaced but had continued to keep his distance.

Crouching down, she retrieved the cellophane wrap for the flowers and stuffed it in her purse along with the bottle. "I'm sorry, I should know better than to make assumptions."

His gaze touched on hers as she straightened, before shifting to a group of mourners drifting past, sweeping the cemetery, with a mechanical precision, as if he was looking for someone. "You've had your own grief to deal with. The military is hard on families."

She frowned. "How did you know that I came from a military family?"

His gaze was suddenly way too percipient, reminding her of just how seductively dangerous O'Halloran could be. The last thing she needed was a reminder that aside from possessing the kind of dark, dangerous good looks that made women go weak at the knees, O'Halloran had another set of traits that had always threatened to melt her on the spot. He liked women. He was solicitous of and ultra-protective of them, and he didn't seem to have a built-in fear of emotional reactions. Nine years ago, after the near miss with the drunk driver, O'Halloran's offer of a shoulder had proved to be her breaking point.

He shrugged. "Your family didn't tell me, they closed ranks. I checked newspaper records and paid a visit to the military base."

"Why?" The question was blunt and just a little rude. She didn't care. Years ago, O'Halloran's failure to find out the most basic facts about her life, his easy defection, had hurt. In that moment, she realized how much she had deceived herself about him. In her heart of hearts, she had wanted him to come after her, to insist that what they had was worth the risk.

"I was worried about you. You were too closed-off, too self-contained. I couldn't figure out why you should be that way. I needed to make sure you were all right."

And suddenly, that night nine years ago was between them; the stifling heat, the edgy emotions, her shattering vulnerability. On the heels of the discovery that, like it or not, she had been carrying some kind of a torch for O'Halloran for nine years, the conversation was abruptly too much.

Glancing at her watch, she picked up her bag and hitched the strap over one shoulder. "I need to go. I'm late for an appointment." She aimed a blank smile somewhere in the direction of his shoulder. "It was good to see you."

And she wished that she hadn't. After her moment with the cover yesterday, she wasn't sure what she felt for O'Halloran. All she knew was that his memory was a lot more manageable than the man himself.

O'Halloran fell into step beside her, making her tense. "I'll walk you to your car." His fingers slid around her wrist, sending a hot, tingling shock down the length of her arm. He turned her palm up, so that the grazing was exposed. "How did that happen?"

Jerking free, she quickened her pace, wincing again as the movement put just a little too much pressure on her knee. Annoyed, Jenna resisted the temptation to rub the knee. The last thing she needed was to invoke O'Halloran's protective instincts.

Although, grimly, she noted that if she had thought

O'Halloran hadn't seen the elastic bandage beneath her leggings, she would be wrong. "Nothing much. As it happens, I had another run-in with a car."

O'Halloran threw her a sharp look, as if he was as surprised as she that she'd touched on a topic that was so closely connected to the hour they'd spent in his apartment making love. But that didn't stop him from firing a string of questions at her as they walked, his voice relaxed and low-key, almost casual, although by the time they reached her car he had mined every salient detail.

"Ticked anyone off lately?"

She found her key and depressed the lock. "Yeah, a fan."

O'Halloran opened the driver's side door, his arm brushing hers as he did so, sending another one of those small electrifying shocks through her. "Are you telling me," he said quietly, "that you think the driver aimed for you?"

Jenna tensed as a replay of the shiny black car heading straight for her at high speed flashed through her mind. "Not exactly, there was no room. If he had swerved he would have hit another car and damaged his own. That's what saved me. I dived between two cars. What bothers me is that he had a long time to see me and he never slowed down."

"It could have been some kid—"

"Playing chicken. I thought of that." Her fingers tightened on the strap of her handbag. "The only problem was it didn't feel like a game."

She took a deep breath. Here was the point where O'Halloran called the men in white coats with the interesting drugs and the padded cell. "Whoever it was, I got the impression he wanted to hit me. Even if he had braked seconds before, he still would have hit me, and he didn't brake."

Instead of dismissing her statement as emotional overreaction, O'Halloran crossed his arms over his chest and seemed content to listen. "And the disgruntled fan? Where does she come in?"

"He," she corrected. "When I got home I found a threatening email."

His expression altered very slightly. Jenna couldn't even say what it was, exactly, that had changed, just that the temperature seemed to drop by several degrees.

Briefly, she outlined the content of the email, omitting her own suspicion that the poisonous fan, aside from being someone from her past, could be somehow linked with Natalie. So far, that part was just a theory, and she didn't want to cause any unnecessary upset. She couldn't forget that O'Halloran had never believed the house fire that had killed Natalie and Jared had been a random arson. According to her aunt, he'd believed that his family had been targeted because he was a cop, and despite leaving the police force, it was an investigation he had never given up.

O'Halloran's gaze settled on her mouth for a pulse-pounding moment. "I'd like to see a copy of the email."

Digging into his pocket, he found his wallet and handed her a card. "You can scan it or fax, or alternatively, drop it by my office."

Battling the sudden warmth in her cheeks and a humming, deepening awareness that was definitely scrambling her brain, she took the card and slipped it into her handbag. The last thing she had expected was that O'Halloran would want any contact with her at all, and the fact that he seemed to want to help her increased the unsettling awareness. "I've deleted the email, but I did keep a print copy. I'll send it to you."

"Did you report the accident?"

"Not to the police. I talked to one of the mall security guys. He was going to check out the parking lot tapes and get back to me."

"What was his name?"

"Mathews."

Another string of questions about the security set-up at the mall and she found herself haemorrhaging more information, including her phone number and email address and eventually handing over Mathews's business card.

She drew a deep breath, feeling suddenly too aware and a whole lot confused. Giving her details to O'Halloran shouldn't have felt like part and parcel of a dating ritual, but suddenly it did. "You don't have to check up on it."

He tucked the card in the pocket of his jeans. "I drive past there on my way to work. It won't hurt to see if Mathews managed to record the licence plate."

O'Halloran held her door as she climbed into her car. The clean, masculine scent of his skin and the faint whiff of some resinous cologne made her stomach clench. Not good!

Stepping back, he lifted a hand as she pulled out of her parking space.

Heart still beating way too rapidly, Jenna couldn't help checking out her rearview mirror. O'Halloran was still studying the mourners gathered in knots and strolling toward cars and she suddenly knew what he was doing at the cemetery.

The dark casual clothes that made him fade into the shadows, the reason there were no flowers.

He wasn't there to mourn; he was surveilling Natalie's grave.

Frowning, Marc watched as Jenna's car merged with traffic.

He had come, as he did every year, to watch the gravesite from a distance and see who visited apart from Natalie's family. Although this year, with a big funeral in progress, the exercise had been a little pointless.

Grimly, he noted that, as with other years, the only bright spot of his vigil had been when Jenna came to place flowers. Now that she had gone, the vigil felt empty.

In point of fact, after blowing his cover so thoroughly, the whole exercise of watching the gravesite was now a waste of time. If the perp had been anywhere near, he would be miles away by now.

Sliding dark glasses onto the bridge of his nose, he turned back to study the cemetery, which was now emptying rapidly. After a few minutes Marc gave up searching for the lean guy wearing the ball cap who had stopped by Natalie's grave.

The man hadn't left anything at the gravesite, or taken anything away; Marc had established that much while he had talked to Jenna. It was possible the man had been seeking out another gravesite and had simply stopped to read the name on Natalie's headstone, but something about him had caught Marc's attention.

Marc was certain he had seen the man before somewhere. He didn't know where or when, but it would come to him.

The moment when Jenna had told him that she had received a threatening email replayed itself, shoving every instinct on high alert.

He didn't like coincidences, and he didn't believe in this one.

There was a connection. He didn't know how, or why, he just knew that in some serpentine way, and after six years, that Jenna held the key to the breakthrough he needed.

Frustration and disbelief held him immobile for long seconds. For years he had meticulously researched every piece of information and evidence connected to both the house fire and the police investigation he had been involved with at the time. He had assumed the motivation for the crime against his family was a revenge attack based on his police work. Now he had to revise that approach.

The thought that the killer had had another motivation entirely was a quantum shift. In his research and briefs to private detectives, he had kept the focus on the criminal family, who were, ironically, because of his personal investigation, now mostly behind bars for a series of other crimes.

He had made the basic error of discounting Natalie's life, and he hadn't factored Jenna in at all. Two mistakes he would now address. He should have examined every aspect of Natalie's life. Jenna, as her cousin and best friend, should have been at the top of his list.

One thing was certain, if Jenna was the key to unlocking the identity of the killer then from now on every part of her life was of interest to him.

The decision to refocus settled in, filling him with a tension that had nothing to do with the investigation and everything to do with Jenna and a past that still tugged at him.

Nine years ago Jenna had attracted, tantalised and frustrated him. When he had found out that she had been an army brat and that she had grown up on military bases here and overseas, she had fallen into context. The ease with which she'd walked away from him when he'd been certain she had wanted him had suddenly made sense. She was used to moving from base to base and never putting roots down. She was used to saying goodbye, and flat out "no." After she had lost a father then a fiancé, she was used to losing, period.

Digging his keys out of his pocket, he strolled toward his truck, which was parked at one end of the lot, out of sight from the main part of the cemetery.

Broodingly he went back over the few minutes he had spent with Jenna. She had been wearing leggings that clung to her slender legs, a hoodie and sneakers, as if she were on her way to the gym.

The clothing was sleek and mouth-wateringly sexy. Like the car she drove, it underlined the changes that had taken place in Jenna's life. Always intriguingly quiet and self-contained, she was now confident and successful, with a sophistication that packed a double punch.

Marc stopped dead as the extent of the attraction humming through him registered.

Damn, he thought mildly. That was something he was going to have to keep a lid on. He couldn't work effectively if he couldn't keep his mind on the job.

Maybe it had been the book he had read last night, and the steamy sex scene, which had shunted him back to the past. Maybe it was just that he was tired of being solitary and alone and his libido was doing the talking.

Whatever was to blame, like it or not, he wanted Jenna Whitmore and, to complicate matters, he was pretty certain she wanted him. He had to consider the likelihood that they would end up in bed, sooner or later.

But first, he had a killer to catch.

Chapter 4

Electrified by the unexpected meeting with O'Halloran, and the taut awareness that seemed to have settled into her bones, Jenna drove to the gym for her usual midafternoon workout. An hour's circuit of exercise machines and weights followed by a shower and she felt physically relaxed. Although the exercise had failed to dislodge the edgy knowledge that kept making her pulse shoot out of control: that, incredibly, despite O'Halloran's low-key manner and cool control, he had been just as aware of her as she had been of him.

When she had finished, Jenna retrieved her bag from her locker, showered, changed and headed for her car.

As she stepped out from beneath the awning that protected the front entrance, her mind still dazedly, sappily fixed on the minutes she'd spent talking to O'Halloran, a scraping sound jerked her head up. She jumped out of the way just as a pot plant came hurtling down from the terrace of one of the apartments over the gymnasium, exploding in a shower of potting mix and terracotta shards on the sidewalk.

One of the trainers, Amanda, a sleek blonde with a lean, toned body, rushed out from the gym. She stared at the splattered remains of what had once been a pretty, trailing geranium. "What happened? Are you okay?"

Jenna brushed soil off one of her shoes. "I'm fine. It missed me by a couple of feet."

Amanda shook her head. "I don't know how it could have fallen. I rent one of those apartments and there's a three-foot wall running along each terrace. The only way anything could fall down was if someone was silly enough to balance a plant on top of the wall."

Stomach tight, chills still running down her spine, Jenna stepped out from the shade into the warmth of the afternoon sunlight and peered upward. If there had been anyone on one of the several terraces directly above her, they were long gone now.

If she had been just a half second faster the pot would have hit her. "Looks like someone was silly enough."

Amanda nudged a terracotta shard with her foot. "What a mess. I'll have a word with Helen. She'll make sure that whoever owns the pot plant knows what happened." She frowned. "You look white as a sheet. You should come inside and sit down, maybe have something to drink."

Jenna backed away, more interested in scanning the apartments above than being soothed, but with the afternoon sun slanting across the windows they looked featureless. At a guess, most of the apartments were empty, since it wasn't quite five. The occupants would still be at work. "No, really, I'm fine and I need to get home." Aiming a blank smile in Amanda's direction, she walked quickly to the car and fumbled the key in the lock.

Glancing in the rearview mirror as she drove to the mall closest to her suburb, she noticed a black Audi following just a little too closely. A small unpleasant jolt almost made her miss the turn.

It was the same type of car that had nearly run her over the previous night. The same car her villain had driven in her latest book.

When the Audi didn't follow her into the parking lot, but instead merged with traffic flowing into the inner city, she let out a shaky breath. The Audi had to be an unnerving coincidence. In a city as large as Auckland, who knew how many of them were zapping around.

She found a space and parked then sat for long moments until her pulse rate returned to normal. She was still unsettled from running into O'Halloran, and on edge in a skittish, feminine way that was utterly at odds with her usual calm control. She was also stressed from the near miss with the pot plant.

When she realized that she was also unconsciously watching the entrance to the parking lot, waiting for the Audi to cruise in, she grabbed her handbag and exited the car.

Paranoia wasn't her favourite state of mind, and she'd already had enough of it in the past twenty-four hours to last her a lifetime.

Looping the strap of her handbag over her shoulder, she strolled into the mall, her stride almost back to her normal, fluid speed now that the workout had loosened up her knee.

Her first port of call was the information kiosk on the ground floor. She asked if Mathews was in and supplied her name. Minutes later, Mathews stepped out of a nearby door.

The conversation was short and to the point. O'Halloran had already called in and they had gone through the security tapes. Mathews handed her a blurred black-and-white print of the parking lot, capturing the Audi close in against the mall building itself. "That's the clearest shot of the car and the plate. Unfortunately, the quality of the cameras isn't great, and the mist further reduced visibility." He shrugged. "A couple of the letters of the plate are visible."

Jenna thanked Mathews and stowed the print in her bag, her pulse once more racing, because O'Halloran *had* come to check on the tapes, proving that he had been serious about helping her. Apparently she had just missed him.

Following her usual track, she called at a number of specialty stores and bought a baked cheesecake to take around to her aunt's for dinner that evening along with a fresh fruit salad and organic yoghurt.

The drive home was uneventful until she took a motorway off ramp and the black Audi cruised up close behind her again.

A horn blared, jerking her gaze back to the road and alerting her to the fact that she was veering into the next lane.

Heart pounding, Jenna corrected her steering then glanced in the mirror to try and see if it was the same car she had seen earlier.

Her stomach tightened at the black colour and the darkly tinted windows, which gave the Audi a menacing aura. Which was exactly what she had intended when she had written about the car in her book.

It looked like the same vehicle, but, unfortunately, she hadn't thought to take the registration number before, so she couldn't confirm that it was.

The car stayed behind her, too close for her to make out the licence plate. The tinted windows meant that beyond a vague, sinister shape she couldn't see the driver.

She changed lanes then glanced in the mirror again as she made the turn, but the Audi had already accelerated away.

Still on edge hours later after she had gotten home from the family dinner, Jenna decided that scanning a copy of the poisonous fan letter and emailing it to O'Halloran could wait until the morning. Spending time with her aunt and two cousins, both of whom were married with children, had been a welcome distraction, but the instant she had gotten in her car to drive home the fear that she would be followed had kicked in. She hadn't, but the possibility had made the drive unpleasant. The last thing she needed to do before bed was add to her tension by rereading the threat.

Walking quickly, she did her nightly round of the locks, checked the alarm was set, made herself a hot drink and climbed the stairs to bed.

Ensconced in the soft nest of duck-down pillows with her Aunt Mary's remedy for sleep, hot milk laced with malt, and the Bible open on her lap at the most comforting section, the Psalms, Jenna tried to relax.

She had a sudden flashback of the pot plant smashing on the pavement.

If she hadn't heard the faint scrape of terracotta

against stone, as if someone had pushed the heavy pot plant, and stopped to look up, she would have been either seriously injured or killed.

The series of unnerving incidents had to be pure coincidence. No one was trying to kill her. Clearly, she had let her imagination run away with her.

Jenna took a sip of hot milk and malt and focused on Psalm thirty-four, deliverance from trouble.

Midnight came and went. She set the empty mug down on her bedside table, replaced the Bible on her nightstand and switched out the light. Turning on her side, she forced her thoughts away from the incident with the pot plant and the malevolent Audi...and her growing conviction that the fan who had written the nasty email was making good on his threat.

Instead, she allowed herself to think about the chance meeting with O'Halloran, and the fact that he had gone to the mall and checked out the security tapes.

The change of focus was instantly soothing. O'Halloran had a rock-solid quality, a take-no-prisoners attitude, when it came to crime and injustice. She had always liked that about him. Somehow, without saying a word, he conveyed an impression of tough, no-holds-barred, protective strength. If he ever got hold of the guy driving the Audi—and she was abruptly certain that it had been a guy, not a woman—she wouldn't want to be in his shoes.

Yawning, she turned over in bed. Her head was swimming with tiredness. As her breathing finally slowed, her thoughts shifted irresistibly back to her first meeting with O'Halloran. Although, nine years ago, she hadn't called him O'Halloran, she had used his first name, Marc.

She had been in her final year at Auckland University and Marc had been taking the same criminal psychology paper she had been studying. They had ended up sitting side by side at a lecture then had gone out for coffee afterward.

The second she had found out he was a cop, she should have made her excuses and left. Instead she had let Marc buy her a second coffee, and introduce her to his friends, two other detectives doing the same course. Still raw and grieving after Dane's death, O'Halloran had somehow slipped beneath her defences. Aware of the dangerous undertow of fascination, she had kept him at arm's-length, promising herself that she would pull back before it was too late. Although, as she'd found out today, controlling O'Halloran and the attraction that had blindsided her hadn't exactly been her strong point.

Frowning, Jenna banished O'Halloran from her thoughts and concentrated on keeping her mind blank until mind-numbing oblivion finally sucked her under.

Aware that she was immersed in a recurring dream, Jenna almost surfaced from a fitful sleep.

She should make herself wake up properly, give herself a good talking to, but the compulsion to drift back into a past that included O'Halloran was unexpectedly powerful. Letting out a breath, she ceased to think. Instead she allowed herself to sink back into the dream, back into the past....

The summer evening was warm enough that she had folded up the gauzy turquoise stole that went with her gown and stuffed it into her evening bag as she hurried out of the hotel ballroom. Stepping into the ladies' room, she checked her reflection in the mirror. Her face was flushed and her hair was definitely mussed. Aside from those details, she looked composed enough, which was a surprise given that she had just won a minor tussle with a date who had suddenly turned from shy and harmless into a ravening octopus.

Jaw set, she hunted in her evening bag, found a spare hairpin and did her best to fix the elegant twist of hair on top of her head. Satisfied that she no longer looked like she'd been dragged backward through a haystack, she made her way to the hotel lobby.

There were no taxis outside the hotel, so she spoke to the concierge. He ordered a taxi but informed her that thanks to a high-profile football game and a rash of conferences, the wait time was half an hour, minimum.

Jenna thanked him. Unwilling to wait in one of the cozy private bars, in case her Jekyll-and-Hyde date came looking for her and added insult to injury by offering her a ride home, she strolled outside to wait.

Twenty minutes later, tired of kicking her heels, she walked back into the lobby to check on the arrival time of the taxi and stopped dead when she saw O'Halloran at the concierge desk.

His back was to her, but there was no mistaking his height, the sleek width of his shoulders or the tough line of his jaw. Heart slamming against her chest, because she was abruptly certain he was looking for her, she turned on her heel and stepped back outside.

Extracting her cell from her evening bag, she tried calling her aunt and uncle, something she had done at approximately five-minute intervals. The call went through to voice mail, signalling that they were still out to dinner with friends. Unfortunately, she hadn't thought to ask which set of friends so she didn't have an alternate number to try.

Slipping the phone back into her bag she glanced at the entrance doors of the hotel and caught another glimpse of O'Halloran as he strolled out of one of the small intimate bars and into another one. Looking for her.

Maybe it was an overreaction, and maybe she was wrong, but instead of waiting a little longer and risking O'Halloran finding her, she started walking. Leaving the hotel on foot wasn't smart, but after the wrench of breaking up with O'Halloran less than two weeks ago, she wasn't about to jeopardise the progress she had made by spending time alone with him.

Aside from the bone-melting attraction, she was acutely aware that despite her efforts to keep things casual they had been on the verge of becoming lovers. The knowledge that she had been a heartbeat away from sleeping with a man she had only known for a few weeks, when she had never come close to sharing that intimacy with Dane, had struck her forcibly.

It had taken courage to make the break with O'Halloran, but it was done, and she wasn't going to complicate the situation by being a wimp now. To cement the decision, she had made arrangements to go overseas. She was newly graduated and free as a bird. She had a friend she could stay with in Sydney and a series of job interviews lined up. She didn't have a clue what she would end up doing for a living, but she flew out in ten days' time.

The decision to leave had filled her with relief. She had read somewhere that one way to neutralise issues and problems—and fatal attractions—was to create geographical distance from them, and she could attest to that fact. Just buying the air ticket had been liberating.

Behind her, she registered footsteps, almost drowned out by the sound of an approaching vehicle. Ahead, warm light flowed from a restaurant. All she needed to do was reach the pooling light and she would be able to ring her uncle again and see if he could come out and pick her up.

She crossed the road, more worried by the footsteps and a potential mugging—or worse—than the car. She was now on a one-way street. The vehicle wouldn't come her way. It would have to veer off at the intersection and continue on downtown.

The sound of the vehicle increased to a roar as, instead of slowing for the intersection, the driver accelerated. Frowning, Jenna glanced over her shoulder. She caught the silhouette of a man as headlights blinded her. It occurred to her that it could be O'Halloran, but all of her attention was taken by the car, which had somehow missed the turn at the intersection and was careering down the one-way street in the wrong direction.

She stepped onto the narrow path that hugged the edge of a bridge. Adrenaline surged when she realized that the man behind her was much closer. She thought he said her name but at that moment the threat from the car became paramount, because the driver appeared to be aiming straight for her.

Dragging at the entangling layers of her skirts, she kicked off her high heels and began to run.

Panic squeezed the breath from her lungs. She needed to reach the end of the bridge and get off the footpath.

She heard her name called again. O'Halloran. Relief coursed through her.

The loud detonation of the vehicle hitting the curb

almost stopped her heart in her chest. Simultaneously an arm snaked around her waist and she found herself lifted up and propelled the last few feet off of the bridge. A split second later, they hit the grassy turf that bordered the stream and the car fish-tailed past, bare inches away, filling her nostrils with the smell of burning rubber and exhaust fumes.

With a second loud thump, the car veered off the path, back onto the road. Headlights glared and a horn sounded as it almost hit a vehicle accelerating down the one-way in the legitimate direction, then sped off into the night.

O'Halloran, who was sprawled over her, shielding her with his body, pushed to his feet and helped her up. "Are you all right?"

Still shaky from the near miss, but oddly elated, crazily, because O'Halloran had noticed that she had left the hotel and had come after her, Jenna found her evening purse, which had landed on the grass a few feet away. "Yes, thanks to you. If you hadn't followed me—"

The glow of a streetlight glanced across taut planes of his face as he handed her her shoes. "You should never have left the hotel on foot. Don't you read the newspapers?"

Jenna fitted one shoe then almost overbalanced as she stepped into the second. With a clipped word, O'Halloran steadied her, and the next minute she was in his arms, pressed hard against the muscled warmth of his chest. "I would have given you a lift," he muttered, then his mouth was on hers.

The passion was hot and instant, and it threw her even more off balance. She had been kissed before by O'Halloran, but it had never felt this needy, this visceral.

Mostly, in the weeks they had dated he had seemed content to let her dictate the pace. As much as she'd appreciated his gentlemanly approach, she had taken that as a sign that she was not in any way special to him. Now, for the first time, she registered that what they had shared had mattered to him, too.

When he would have pulled back, she cupped his neck and held him there, leaning into the hard planes and angles of his body. Long seconds passed, and eventually he lifted his head, his gaze narrowed and glittering. "Do you want me to take you home, or do you want to come with me?"

The question hung in the air, raw and edged. Her throat felt thick, her chest tight. She knew what he was offering. She could be with him now, for the night: no strings.

The thought that after tonight she would probably never see O'Halloran again, that this could be her last chance with him, touched a chord somewhere deep inside her. Fierceness and longing welled up, gripping her so tightly she could barely breathe.

The idea that they could be together was both hurtful and mesmerisingly, impossibly tempting. She wanted O'Halloran, that had never been at issue. And she was leaving soon, so there was no danger that she would be tempted to cling.

Before she could reason it out any further, and remember all of the factors that added up to a *no*, she said, "Yes, I want to come with you."

Half an hour later they reached his apartment. O'Halloran didn't bother to switch on a light. He simply tossed his car keys on a hall table, pulled her into his arms and kissed her for long, drugging minutes.

Shrugging out of his jacket, he pulled her into a sitting room lit by moonlight streaming through French doors.

Winding her arms around his neck, Jenna went up on her toes and angled her chin for his kiss. She could feel the ridge of his arousal against one hip, the rough glide of O'Halloran's palms on her naked back.

She jerked at his tie and unfastened buttons and felt the zipper on her gown give way, the soft slide of fabric as the halter-neck tie at her nape released and her dress puddled on the floor. With a stifled groan, O'Halloran dipped his head and took one breast into his mouth and the night turned molten.

Long seconds later the world tilted sideways as she found herself swung into O'Halloran's arms then set down on a couch, the leather cool against her back.

O'Halloran came down beside her and she pulled him close, loving the heat blasting off his big body, the flagrant sensuality of his skin against hers, the masculine weight and scent of him. Somewhere outside, music played in the distance, a slow, languorous beat that seemed to permeate the night as she ran her palms down the long, muscular line of his back.

She felt his fingers tugging at the waistband of her panties, then she was completely naked. Fumbling at the fastening of O'Halloran's pants, she dragged the zipper down and felt him hot and silky in her hands.

With a stifled sound, O'Halloran's hand stayed hers. Impatiently, he finished undressing. Moonlight gleamed on jet-black hair, the sleek muscularity of broad shoulders as he came down between her legs.

When O'Halloran finally sheathed himself and slid inside her, the moment was primal and extreme. She logged his flare of surprise at the difficulty of penetration, the question in his eyes, then his mouth came down on hers and she ceased to think as the night dissolved....

Jenna came out of sleep, her heart pounding, her skin drenched with perspiration. She blinked, for the briefest of moments unable to separate the dream from reality. She could still feel the touch of O'Halloran's hands, his mouth, the weight of his body pressing down on hers....

Taking a steadying breath, she studied the confines of her room—the dim outline of her bedroom dresser, the moulded rose on the ceiling—in an effort to reorient herself.

She hadn't dreamed about making love with O'Halloran in years, although she guessed after her emotional episode with the book cover, she should have expected her subconscious to throw her a curveball. That revelation reinforced by her sharply physical response to O'Halloran at the cemetery had reignited the inconvenient, simmering attraction.

It was there, a part of her, whether she liked it or not, and now she had to deal with it. Despite writing any number of agonising scenes dealing with the exact same romantic problem, she had no earthly clue how she could nullify it in herself. Theory was all very well, the only problem was her body didn't seem to respond to logic.

Climbing out of the entangling sheets, she walked to the window, drew back the curtain and stared out into her back garden. Cold seemed to press through the glass, making her shiver.

The accident had featured in her dream also.

Her too-creative mind had obviously resurrected the old incident, because of what had happened the previous night. As frightening as it had been at the time, she had never considered that the almost-accident nine years ago had been anything more than some drunk driver who had lost control of his, or her, vehicle.

She had certainly never thought that it might have been a deliberate attempt to kill her.

Although there was a curious symmetry to the events that kept popping into her mind. O'Halloran had featured in both. He had been there to save her nine years ago; now, suddenly, he was back in the picture again.

She had a brief flash of the moment in the cemetery when his gaze had dropped to her mouth.

Heat pooled low in her stomach when she considered the fact that, nine years on, she still wanted O'Halloran, and he wanted her.

She rubbed at the goose-flesh that decorated her arms and stared blindly at the moonlight-washed garden.

The thought made her stomach knot and her heart pound. She was twenty-nine, almost thirty, successful at what she did and calmly in control of her life. She shouldn't be so affected by a simple physical attraction—by chemistry. But it seemed that where O'Halloran was concerned nothing was simple.

For years, she had buried her head in the sand and lived a life devoid of emotional and physical intimacy. She hadn't questioned her refusal to sleep with any of the men she had dated, or her preference to remain single, she had simply put it down to her perfectionist streak and isolating career.

But in the space of little more than a day, that had all changed. After years of living alone, eating alone and sleeping alone, she wanted what other women took for granted. She wanted a husband who loved her, the closeness and the intimacy and the heart-pounding sex, and she wanted them with a fierceness that seemed to be growing by the minute.

To compound her madness, she didn't just want those things with some misty, as-yet-unidentified man. She wanted them with O'Halloran.

The following day, after getting more and more annoyed every time she thought about the encounters with the black Audi, and with the blurred mall photograph and the misspelt email tucked into her handbag, Jenna walked into the Auckland Central police station.

She had spent the past two hours doing radio interviews, so she was dressed for business in a charcoal-grey jacket and skirt, with red accessories, a sleek pair of heels and matching bag. Maybe what she was wearing shouldn't matter because she was there to report a crime, but she figured with the weirdness factor of being stalked by a fan, she needed every bit of credibility she could scrape up.

After waiting for a good twenty minutes, she took a seat opposite the detective she had been assigned.

Detective Farrell, a slim, attractive brunette, her desk swamped with files, was dismissive. Harassment in the form of a disgruntled email from a fan, which did not contain any concrete threat, and Jenna's suspicion that she was being followed by someone driving a black Audi, were not strong enough evidence to justify any further action. The reason she had seen the Audi on a number of occasions was probably because the person who drove the car lived nearby.

Keeping her cool, Jenna explained that the car was the same make and model she had used in her latest book and, to compound things, the same type of car that had almost run her over in the mall parking lot. Briefly, she related the incident with the pot plant outside her gym, and her conclusion that she was being stalked.

Farrell's gaze sharpened at that. She took details, asked Jenna to fill out an official complaint then promised to put a detective on the case, although they couldn't help with extra security for her upcoming book tour. "We'll certainly look into the allegation of stalking, but until we get something more concrete I can't commit man hours solely for protection. If we can trace this car or collect evidence of a crime like vandalism or a break-in then the picture changes. If you're worried, you should arrange security for your tour."

Farrell rose to her feet, indicating that the interview was over. She apologised that they couldn't do more up front, but with a mini crime wave on their hands in the form of a gang war and a manhunt for a serial arsonist, they were already short-handed.

Jenna thanked Farrell for her time as she packed away the email. The interview had gone as she had expected, but she'd had to try. With a publicity tour for *Deadly Valentine* beginning in just two days, she had hoped the police would at least provide her with protection for the signings. Most of them were in large department stores and were well-publicised. With crowds of shoppers milling around, they were obvious venues for a stalker.

As she stood up to leave, Farrell's gaze sharpened.

"You're Natalie O'Halloran's cousin, right? I used to be Marc's partner. How's he going with his new business?"

The mention of O'Halloran sent a small tingling shock through her. Jenna's cheeks warmed as she fielded the enquiry using the odd snippets of information that her aunt had let slip.

The yawning gap in her knowledge about O'Halloran added to her sense of disorientation. She wanted O'Halloran, and the intensity of the attraction and the sudden U-turn she had made were just a little bit scary. Especially when she considered that what she knew about his present life would fit on the back of a postage stamp.

Although, that would soon all change, since he was her next port of call.

Chapter 5

Jenna strolled into the sleek offices of VIP Security and made an enquiry at the front desk. A short phone call later, the pretty redhead showed her through to O'Halloran's office.

Dressed in a suit with a crisp white shirt and blue tie, O'Halloran was standing in front of a large bank of windows, a cell to one ear, his back to the expansive view of the harbour. Jenna disguised a sudden attack of nerves by glancing around the large, cleanly furnished office.

Now that she was here, she couldn't help feeling a little pushy and intrusive. Worse, she was beginning to feel that she had imagined O'Halloran's interest, and that his protective behaviour was simply a knee-jerk reaction he would have toward any woman in trouble.

His gaze neutral, he terminated his conversation and

indicated she should sit in one of the comfortable leather armchairs grouped around a coffee table.

Dragging her gaze from the way his jacket fitted the broad width of his shoulders, Jenna sat down.

Instead of taking the chair opposite, he walked to his desk and picked up a file. "I checked out the numbers I could get off the plates of the Audi and came up with a list." He extracted a sheet of paper from the file and handed it to her. "Do you recognise any names?"

She studied the list, which included personal and company names, and shook her head. "Sorry, no."

She rummaged in her bag and extracted the folded email she had promised to give him. As she did so a small journal fell out, flipping open at a page of ideas she had jotted down for the book on which she was currently working.

O'Halloran retrieved the journal and seemed instantly riveted by the lines of neat print. He handed it back to her. "Notes for your next book?"

Jenna stuffed the journal back in her handbag. At least that answered any question about whether or not O'Halloran knew what she did for a living. "It's my current work in progress. It should be on the shelves in about eighteen months."

To cover the suddenly awkward silence, she handed O'Halloran the email. "I didn't know you knew I wrote."

O'Halloran, apparently absorbed by the printed email she'd given him, took the leather chair opposite. "Mary told me when you sold your first book."

Of course. The wild speculation that O'Halloran could have read one of her books died. She didn't know why she hadn't thought of that before. Aunt Mary was inordinately proud of the fact that she had gotten published.

O'Halloran frowned. "How many times has this guy written to you?"

Relieved, Jenna grabbed at the new direction of the conversation. "Just once, as far as I know. I did a check of all of my email files and I can't find anything else from that address."

O'Halloran frowned. "Have you taken this to the police?"

"I've just come from Auckland Central. A Detective Farrell's making enquiries."

His gaze sharpened. "Elaine Farrell's a good cop. If anyone can track this guy down, she can."

"But not you?"

"That wasn't what I said."

Relief washed through her—for a minute there she had thought O'Halloran was going to back away from helping her. Too wired to sit, Jenna rose to her feet and walked to the window. "Good, because someone's playing games with me, and I'm not entirely sure why. If it's the poisonous fan, then the motivation doesn't quite stack up. He says he wants me to take the book off the market, but the fact is I don't have the power to do that. Plus, there's one other thing."

A relevant fact she hadn't been able to elaborate on with Detective Farrell after her reaction to Jenna's statement that the stalker was using the same car as the villain in her book. "The fan who's stalking me is using details from my latest book."

"The Audi?"

She shot O'Halloran a startled look, surprised that he had made the connection with the Audi so quickly.

He looked neither incredulous nor disbelieving, which was a relief, because she badly needed someone to believe her.

Walking back to her seat, she sat down. "That's right. The villain in *Deadly Valentine* drove a black Audi. He used it to creep Sara out." She cleared her throat. "Sara is the name of my heroine."

Firming her jaw she decided there was no point in not revealing the entire embarrassing truth. "And that's not all." She was suddenly glad she was sitting, not standing. "I based Sara on myself."

"Her character?"

"And her schedule. Normally, Sara, as a private detective, is involved in investigations. In *Deadly Valentine* she tries to take time off from solving cases to write a book. I used my daily routine, including my writing hours and all of my weekly appointments, as a model for Sara's schedule."

"You could change your routine."

"I have, now. The problem is, I think he managed to track me down to the gym I use and followed me home from there, so I'm pretty sure he now knows where I live."

O'Halloran's head came up. "Have you noticed anyone suspicious near your house?"

Relief flooded her. O'Halloran's instant acceptance of her situation convinced her that she had done the right thing in approaching him. Farrell had been efficient, but Jenna knew for a fact that when O'Halloran had been a cop, his instincts and his reputation for capturing criminals had been second to none. "Not yet." And she had been looking. "An even bigger problem is that I have a book-signing tour planned in a couple of days. All of the venues are well-advertised. Whether I change my routine or not, it now doesn't matter, he can still find me."

There was no easy way to say it. All she could do was be blunt. "That's the reason I'm here, I need protection."

Marc gave himself a mental shake, and forced himself to concentrate on what Jenna was saying rather than the shadowy hint of cleavage in the vee of her jacket and the ultra-sexy red heels, which made her legs look even longer and more elegant. In point of fact, he never ogled women when they came into his office. Business was business and separate from his after-hours life. As both a cop and a bodyguard he occasionally had to offer comfort to women, which he was good for, but he had never been tempted to cross the line into the personal.

Until now.

Grimly, he ignored the tension that had gripped him the instant Jenna had walked into his office and the uncomfortable pressure of his semi-aroused state. If he hadn't been entirely convinced about Jenna's reasons for thinking she was being stalked, the look on her face would have been enough. She was genuinely concerned, and with some of the weirdos that were around—especially online weirdos—she should be. With the growing hype around Jenna's books, the signings would be packed out. "You look like you could use something to drink. What would you like, coffee? Tea? Or something cold?"

Jenna opted for coffee, with sugar, so he walked out to the dispenser in the hall and got two coffees. By the time he returned, she was out of her seat and investigating some of the books that lined one wall.

Against the plain cream decor, she stood out like an

exotic orchid in her dark suit and red shoes. The charcoal grey of the suit, which should have looked boring and a little nerdy, was somehow transformed by the sexy cut that clung to every delicate curve.

Jaw tightening at the sudden raft of memories, he set the coffee down.

Jenna slipped a book on criminal psychology she'd been examining back in the case. "I see you're still interested in detective work."

He saw the moment she registered that maybe the topic wasn't a happy one.

"I'm sorry," she said quietly. "You must miss detective work, you were passionate about it."

He shrugged. "I still am, but I've got other focuses now." Detective work had cost him his wife and child. From that point on, he had learned to temper the idealistic streak that had driven him so hard.

He was still black and white with his ideals. As far as he was concerned, justice was clear cut. If you did the crime then you deserved to do the time. Stepping out of the job had been a wrench, but overall it had been good for him. Leaving the force had also carried the bonus of allowing him to continue with his private investigation into the crime that had killed his family, a situation that had caused a lot of friction with his superior officer.

The edgy highs and lows were absent from his security work, but he didn't miss the seamier side of life, the drunks or the narcs. Overall he had learned to live with the challenge of co-owning the security business.

Strolling over to his desk, Marc picked up his phone. "Private protection is a good option. With the shortage of police staffing, Farrell would probably be stretched to provide protection unless you received a threat that involved physical harm."

Jenna crossed her arms over her chest and stared out of his window. "Can we not talk about Detective Farrell, please?"

O'Halloran was silent for a beat as he absorbed the subtext. Farrell was a good cop, but her bedside manner left something to be desired. He had never minded her abrasiveness. It had worked for him, because the last thing he had needed was a female partner who wanted more than just a professional relationship. Besides, he figured Farrell's manner was a coping mechanism. "VIP protection is expensive."

"I can afford it. I have a list of dates and the locations of the book signings." She dug in her handbag and handed him a sheet of paper. "We'll need to stay away, but that's no problem. Naturally, I'll pay all travel and hotel costs. Like I said, I can afford it."

Marc noted Jenna's use of *we* as if she assumed he was going to bodyguard her personally. The increased heat in his loins underlined the reason why that was not a good idea. "I'll have to check with my partner and see who we've got available."

Jenna's gaze locked with his, and the flash of hurt in her eyes made him feel like a heel. "Of course."

Marc stepped into Ben McCabe's office. McCabe, an ex-member of the New Zealand Special Forces, the Special Air Service, was on a call and looked harassed.

He finished the call and checked his watch. "I'm out of here. Gotta pick up the kids from school today."

Marc steeled himself against the subject of kids. He didn't often allow himself to think about the son he had lost in the house fire, but he couldn't ignore the small painful fact that if Jared had lived, he would have been a similar age to McCabe's small son. "I know we're committed with the art exhibition at the museum but I need a guy. Who's on standby?"

McCabe slipped his laptop into a briefcase and checked his watch again. Since his wife was a high-profile member of the mega-wealthy Lombard hotelier family, security for his family was always a burning issue. "For the next week, no one. Howard and Burke are on vacation, Kinsella's off sick. Why?"

"I've got Jenna Whitmore in my office."

McCabe frowned as he slipped his cell phone into his pocket. "The name's familiar."

"She's a novelist."

McCabe's expression cleared. "I saw her on TV a couple of weeks ago. She writes romance novels. My wife reads them."

"Romantic suspense, actually."

McCabe's blank expression informed Marc that he shouldn't have bothered to make the distinction. "She needs protection for her upcoming book tour."

McCabe looked distracted as he searched the surface of his desk. "Then you're going to have to do it, because there isn't anyone else."

Marc's jaw firmed. "What about you? I could take your place at the museum job."

McCabe found his car keys. "And art's a lot more straightforward than personal bodyguarding? Sorry." He sent Marc a rueful grin. "Jenna Whitmore is female. Even if I had the time, which I don't, Roma would have me hung, drawn and quartered if I even mentioned that

I was thinking about guarding a young, single woman. You'll have to do it."

Another flash of heat went through Marc at the thought of spending several days in close quarters with Jenna. He had decided he wanted Jenna, and it was a fact that he needed to stay close to her because he was certain that she was connected with the killer he was hunting. But the last thing he needed was the distraction of a sexual liaison, at least not yet. When they went to bed this time, he wanted to take things slow and easy. Nine years ago he had given in to adrenaline, and the jealousy that had seared him when he had found out, just days after their break-up, that Jenna was dating someone else. Not quite a cop, but close. A police recruit who had taken the same criminal psychology paper. Consequently, he had rushed her and for a woman like Jenna, it had been the wrong approach.

His jaw tightened. That sealed his decision. "I have priorities. Protecting Jenna Whitmore isn't one of them."

For one thing, with McCabe based at the museum for the next few days, supervising the security for the high-profile art exhibition, and every other able-bodied employee contracted out, he was more or less tied to the office. Problem solved. Jenna would have to approach another security firm.

Marc heard a whisper of sound behind him. Frowning, he checked the door. The corridor appeared to be empty.

McCabe snapped his fingers, as if he'd just had a light-bulb moment. He dropped his briefcase back on the desk. "There is a solution if you want it. Phillips can do office duty."

He opened a drawer and pulled out an address book. Flipping through, he found a number, scribbled it on the back of a business card and handed it to Marc. "He's staying at an apartment down on the viaduct, but he's not a happy camper. Give him a call, I guarantee he'll be in the office before you put the phone down."

Marc took the card. The option was viable. Phillips, an ultra-fit adrenaline junkie who had broken his arm rock-climbing, had been constantly wandering into the office like a lost soul, complaining that he hated the downtime. Another ex-cop, he was more than qualified to cover in the office over the next week.

McCabe grabbed his jacket and briefcase and headed for the door. He frowned. "Jenna Whitmore? Didn't you used to know her?"

"She's a cousin of my wife."

McCabe looked briefly arrested. "The woman you used to date?"

Marc's brows jerked together. "How did you know about that?"

McCabe lifted a brow. "This is a security firm."

With a sense of resignation, Marc slipped the card with Phillips's address into his pocket. He should have guessed. He had done a thorough background check on McCabe before he had bought into the business. It made sense that McCabe had been just as cautious. "We were just good friends."

McCabe's smile was enigmatic. "Sure. Don't break the company rule."

After McCabe's fall from grace when he had guarded Roma Lombard, who was now his wife, Marc figured there was only one hard and fast rule.

Be sure before you sleep with the client.

Chapter 6

I have priorities. Protecting Jenna Whitmore isn't one of them.

After using the facilities in the ladies' room, Jenna washed her hands and yanked a paper towel from the dispenser. In the process, the dispenser flopped open and a pile of towels cascaded onto the floor.

Muttering beneath her breath at the obviously faulty piece of equipment, she jammed the bunch of excess towels back into the top of the dispenser and closed the unit. It didn't look right, but there was nothing she could do about that.

Feeling increasingly irritable, hurt and mortified, she dried her hands on the one towel she had kept for herself then tossed it into the trash.

Balancing her handbag on the counter, she took time

out to apply fresh lip gloss and control the burst of anger and hurt. She didn't normally lose her temper.

Although that was because she was literally tied to her computer in her own home. No one else lived there, so of course there was no one to get mad at.

Feeling even more annoyed, with her life as well as with O'Halloran, she took another calming breath and strolled back to O'Halloran's office, bracing herself to be, at the very least, neutral.

There was no need. When she walked into his office, O'Halloran was talking on the phone again. The sun slanting through the window accentuated the clean lines of his profile, his rock-solid jaw. While she'd been in the bathroom, he had taken off his jacket and rolled up his sleeves. She dragged her gaze away from tanned, muscled biceps.

She couldn't help noticing that he looked fit and toned, as if he worked out. She guessed if he still personally took on VIP protection jobs for selected clients, a high level of fitness would be required.

Seconds later, he ended his conversation and strolled back to his desk. Too upset to sit, Jenna avoided his gaze and concentrated, instead, on a series of framed certificates on the wall. She remembered with a jolt that O'Halloran had qualified as a lawyer before he had applied for the police college.

O'Halloran's expression was remote as he produced a sheaf of papers. Jaw tight, she wondered who he had managed to get to protect her.

"We can offer you our VIP protection service for the period of your book-signing tour, but before we go ahead with the paperwork I'm going to have to ask you a few personal questions."

"Maybe I can shorten the process. I live alone, and I don't have any pets or lovers. I do not have a current relationship."

Come to that, she didn't have a recent-past one, either. Not that it was any of O'Halloran's business that the only man who had been on her personal horizon for the past few years was a man she had never met. She didn't even know what her number-one fan, Lydell88, looked like since he had never supplied a photograph.

With a shrug, he handed her the agreement. "You sound like you know your way around a protection contract."

Jenna took the sheets. "I had to research VIP protection for one of my books so I rang up a security firm. They were happy to tell me about their business and gave me a sample contract."

Dropping her handbag on the floor, she sat and examined the pages. The print was just a shade too small for comfort. Automatically, she reached for her spectacles, then froze.

It was a small thing, but there was no way she was going to allow O'Halloran to see her wearing spectacles. She had gone to a lot of trouble with her outfit and her make-up. She wasn't going to ruin it all now with a pair of nerdy glasses.

"If the print is too small, I can get Melanie to dig out a large-print version."

She pretended not to hear the question. "This looks complicated."

His rueful grin made her stomach tense.

"People are always complicated."

She lifted the sheets a fraction closer, trying to ignore the crazy hit of attraction. Men who didn't want you around, even when you were prepared to pay them, shouldn't be attractive. "As opposed to art. That's pretty straightforward."

O'Halloran's brows jerked together. "I knew it. You heard."

Jenna tried for a distracted look, which wasn't hard since she was trying to read the tiny print without squinting. "Heard what?"

"What I said in McCabe's office."

His narrowed gaze skewered hers. With an effort of will Jenna dragged her gaze free and tried to ignore her crazy, automatic response.

She turned a page. "McCabe. That would be the tall, good-looking one."

O'Halloran crossed his arms over his chest. "I don't tend to think of him that way, but we're probably talking about the same guy."

She gave up on trying to read a contract she could barely see and gave him the kind of steely glance she usually reserved for the marketing people when they messed with her covers. "All I need is a bodyguard for a few days. If you don't want to take on the job, fine. I'm sure you'll have someone who can."

"You're upset."

"Not in the least."

"Good. Then shall we get down to business?"

Minutes later, after O'Halloran had gone through the agreement clause by clause, underlining the disconcerting fact that even if he hadn't chosen law as a career he had all the attributes of a lawyer, Jenna signed.

She placed the pen beside the contract, folded her copy and tucked it into her handbag. "I'm sure, whoever this mystery bodyguard is, he'll be excellent at the job."

A knock on the door broke the simmering tension. A tanned, muscular man, who looked like he had just walked in off the beach or a ski slope, entered the room. Despite the fact that one arm was encased in plaster, he could have been a poster boy for a bodyguard movie.

O'Halloran introduced Troy Phillips.

Jenna shook Phillips's hand. When he smiled, he was even more dazzling. She couldn't help thinking that if he was her protection at her book signings, which were overrun with women of all ages, he was the one who was going to be mobbed.

Grimly, Marc propped himself against his desk and noted the interested gleam in Phillips's gaze and Jenna's response.

It was a watershed moment. Jenna was single, attractive, vulnerable and his.

Despite his reservations, he couldn't allow anyone else to protect her for the simple reason that he didn't want any other man that close to her.

If he'd had any doubts that he was involved with Jenna, they would have crashed and burned in that moment. If Phillips had been fit and ready for duty, instead of here to answer calls and shuffle through some paperwork, there would be no way he would let him near her.

Jenna sent him a coolly professional glance that grated, and agreed to be in touch about exact travel dates and times.

Aware that he had been expertly dismissed, Marc followed her out into the corridor then punched the call button on the elevator.

Jenna glanced at a colourful abstract painting, which decorated the wall opposite. "Phillips certainly looks fit."

Marc folded his arms across his chest. "He could probably handle just about anything with one arm tied behind his back, but he's not on active duty at the moment. It's not our policy to assign security personnel with broken limbs to a job."

He saw the wariness in Jenna's gaze and could have kicked himself. He had put that look there. She knew he had been looking for someone else to guard her, although not the reason why. If he could take back those moments he would.

The elevator doors slid open. She sent him a fierce glance as she stepped into the elevator. "Then who is?"

Marc muttered an imprecation beneath his breath, held the door before it closed and stepped inside the elevator. "Who do you think? I am."

"You said you didn't want to do the security."

"For good reasons. Personal reasons."

The flare of surprise in her eyes made his chest tighten. Cupping her jaw, he dipped his head, giving her time to pull back if she wanted. He was taking a risk in kissing Jenna. He couldn't rule out the fact that he had completely misread the situation; it had happened before.

He caught the startled moment of eye contact, the faint hitch in her breathing, then his mouth brushed hers once, twice, then settled more firmly.

Heat and sensation shot through him. Images of that long-ago night rose up to haunt him as she lifted up on her toes and angled her jaw to deepen the kiss. His phone vibrated, breaking the moment. Reluctantly lifting his head, Marc forced himself to release her and step back out into the hall.

As the doors slid closed on the elevator, he squashed

the urge to take the stairs and continue the conversation down in the lobby. Although it wasn't exactly a conversation that he wanted anymore, and now Jenna knew it.

Checking his phone and opting to leave the call, he strolled back to his office, although his mind was no longer on work.

It had been nine years since he had dated Jenna. A lot of water had passed under the proverbial bridge since then, but one thing was still true.

Whether she was dressed in jeans and oversized shirts, her long hair loose, or encased in a sexy, sophisticated suit with heels, the qualities that had originally drawn him were the same.

She had been funny, ultra-smart and sweet, with an intriguing bluntness that had been refreshing. She had also seemed to get his cop humour and she hadn't blinked an eye when he'd had to carry a weapon, something that actively frightened most women. He guessed that coming from a military family showed.

He had wanted more—a lot more—than the casual dating that had seemed to suit her, but the second he had pushed she had closed down. He had accepted the rejection. He hadn't wanted to let her go, but he had moved on. Almost ten years on she had developed some complex, fascinating layers that hooked him in even harder.

And the attraction wasn't all one way. The kiss, at least, had proved that.

Which was a relief because this time he wasn't prepared to cut his losses and step back.

Jenna drove to her local cinema to watch her usual five o'clock movie, but she could barely concentrate on traffic.

The kiss with O'Halloran replayed itself, making her toes curl and almost making her miss her turn.

The acute awareness that had held her in a vice-like grip as the elevator door had closed gripped her again, along with a dose of sheer, feminine panic. She had dreamed about making love with O'Halloran. She'd had trouble not thinking about him for most of the day, but in the space of a few seconds, the kiss had changed everything. It had been a statement of intent and a claim.

O'Halloran hadn't wanted to guard her because he had wanted to keep work and his personal life separate.

The thought that O'Halloran now considered her to be part of his personal life sent another wave of heat through her.

Whether she was ready or not, it was too late: they were involved.

She parked in the gloomy underground parking area at the mall, locked the car and remembered to make a note of anyone around her. She found her phone, which had a very good camera, and carried it in her hand as she walked into the building. If anything untoward happened, she was determined to at least take a photo of whoever she thought might be following her.

She bought her ticket then spent a few minutes sitting in the cinema lobby, observing people coming and going. Five minutes before her movie was scheduled to start, she walked into the now dim cinema and headed for *her* seat.

She liked to sit near the front, because the seats were less popular, so she usually always got the middle seat, and often no one else occupied the row. The front row also gave the illusion of almost being in the movie, which added to the experience.

As she walked toward her favourite seat, something white attracted her attention. At first she thought it was a piece of rubbish on the seat that the cinema staff had failed to clear away.

But the scent of roses hit her and suddenly her skin was crawling.

A single white rose was placed neatly on the seat that she usually occupied, if no one else had claimed it.

The scene could have been cut from *Deadly Valentine*.

A single white rose had been the calling card of the villain who had stalked Sara.

Chapter 7

Spine tingling, because whoever was stalking her had been here just minutes ago, and could still be in the theatre, *watching her*, Jenna walked quickly to the side aisle and forced herself to skim the ranks of seats and study faces.

The theatre wasn't packed. The movie was part of an arts festival program, so had limited appeal. Something about a balding head and the glint of spectacles sparked a memory. She lifted her camera to take a picture. At that moment the lights went out and sound thundered from the stereo system. Startled, she inadvertently pressed the shutter as the phone slipped from her fingers. The flash temporarily blinded her.

Someone uttered a short, uncomplimentary phrase. By the time she had found the phone and located where the balding man had been sitting, he was gone.

Her mouth was dry, her heart hammering. Tension zinged through her. She didn't know why she had singled him out, some detail had alerted her. She could have been wrong, but if so, why had he left?

Ignoring the incensed glances being sent her way, and the fact that a member of the cinema staff, with flashlight in hand, was heading straight for her, she walked quickly back to the seat that had the rose neatly placed on it. Crouching down, she took another photo. As she did so she noticed that the rose had a piece of clear cellophane wrapped around it at the base and a white ribbon.

Rising to her feet, she apologised to the teenage boy with the flashlight and agreed that she was leaving. Repressing a shudder, she picked the rose up by the flower head so that she wouldn't touch either the stem, cellophane or the ribbon.

As far as Jenna was concerned the rose was evidence. It was a long shot, but it was possible that a verifiable fingerprint might be found on the wrapping. In terms of getting a conviction, there would probably be no gain, but if she could identify the perpetrator then that would most likely stop him from stalking her.

Minutes later, she walked back out into daylight. Unlocking her car, she placed the rose carefully on the passenger seat. Reaching into her purse, she found the business card O'Halloran had given her.

Fingers a little unsteady, she pressed in his number and waited for him to pick up.

The calm timbre of his voice was reassuring. Taking a deep breath, she made an effort to speak slowly and deliberately. "He was here, at the movies. He left a rose on my seat."

The tension in her voice must have alerted him, because he didn't ask any questions about the rose. "Are you all right?"

"I'm fine." She drew an impeded breath. "I saw him."

There was a brief silence, although in no way did Jenna get the sense that O'Halloran was either still or contemplative. She got the impression that he was moving, fast. "Does he know that you saw him?"

"I think so, since my camera flash went off in his eyes."

There was another silence punctuated by a muffled thud as if a car door had just been pulled shut. "Where are you now?"

Jenna gave him directions to the mall. Satisfaction took the edge off the adrenaline rush as she heard the sound of O'Halloran's vehicle accelerating.

"Get in your car, lock the doors. I'll be there in ten minutes. If you see him again, get out of there and call me."

"I haven't seen him since I left the cinema."

"Good. Ten minutes."

Feeling shaky, mostly from the adrenaline that had been shooting through her system ever since she had spotted the rose, Jenna hung up and locked herself in her car.

As tempted as she was to watch the entrances to the parking lot for O'Halloran's arrival, she forced herself to watch the mall entrance. There were four entrances, so the chances that her stalker would come out of this one—if he was still in the mall—would be small. But if a bald man came out there was a possibility she could get another picture, maybe even a car registration.

That thought reminded her about the photos she had

taken in the cinema. Thumbing through the menu of her phone she brought up the two photos.

There was a clear shot of the white rose. The other, ruined by the odd angle caused by her losing her grip on the phone, showed a man with his hand up, as if he didn't want his photo taken.

The faint, sweet scent of the rose filled the interior of the car as she stared at the indistinct image. A creepy, tingling sensation swept the length of her spine.

It was him, she was certain of it. Although, who he was she had no idea, because his facial features were almost entirely obscured. All she had was an indication of age, somewhere in his thirties or forties, the fact that he was bald and wore glasses.

It wasn't a lot to go on, but it was *something*, even if the police wouldn't recognise it as concrete evidence.

A sleek, dark truck slid into the space next to her.

O'Halloran levered himself out from behind the wheel. Emotion, impulsive and almost overwhelming, swept through Jenna as she unlocked her car and climbed out. The irritations and disappointments of their earlier meeting—the searing moment when he had kissed her—dissolved in a rush. O'Halloran had turned up and he was forgiven.

Crazily, she felt like throwing herself into his arms. Her jaw clenched against the desire. After what had happened in the elevator that would be the equivalent of giving O'Halloran a green light and she hadn't had time to think that far ahead yet.

O'Halloran strode around the side of her car and gripped her shoulders. "Are you all right?"

"I'm fine, I managed to get the ro—"

The sentence was smothered against O'Halloran's

muscled shoulder as he pulled her close for a dizzying few seconds. Palms flattened against the hard wall of his chest, she registered the heat of his body, the clean, male scent of him, the faint resinous scent of cologne.

O'Halloran's gaze locked with hers, for a breathless moment she thought he was going to kiss her again, then she was free.

He dragged his fingers through his hair and avoided her gaze, as if he needed a few seconds. "Let's see the photo you took."

"He was sitting in the cinema. It was dark, so the shot is not great." She reached back into the car, found her phone and brought up the last two shots.

As O'Halloran studied both photos, it fleetingly registered once again that he hadn't questioned her panic over the rose, which struck Jenna as odd. After all, there were a number of innocent reasons for a rose to be left behind. The most obvious was that it had been a dating gift left behind by mistake. Although, Jenna was certain that if she was ever offered a rose on a date she wouldn't forget it.

O'Halloran frowned as he studied the indistinct shot of the man with his hand up, covering his face. "What makes you so sure it's him?"

She rubbed her arms. "I'm not sure. I just thought that the guy who left the rose might still be in the cinema, waiting to catch my reaction. When I looked up, *he* was watching me."

"Did he approach you?"

The remote quality of O'Halloran's gaze, the terse, incisive questions, made her stiffen. If she hadn't known that he had once been a cop, she would know now. "No. I was asked to leave by one of the cinema staff. The next time I checked back in his direction he was gone. But I got the rose."

She opened her car door, and indicated the white rose nestled on the passenger seat. O'Halloran's expression didn't change, but she felt like the temperature had just dropped by a couple of degrees.

"Have you touched the cellophane?"

"I picked it up by the flower head."

"Good girl. Was there a card?"

"No. Nothing." An automatic shudder went through her. The villain hadn't attached a card in *Deadly Valentine*, either, because the rose itself had been both message and threat, signalling that the villain had never forgotten Sara's rejection of him.

"Wait in the car. I'll be a few minutes."

"If you think I'm following that order you can forget it." Jenna grabbed her handbag and locked her car. She didn't want to stay behind in the car being creeped out by the rose for one more second. "I'm coming with you."

O'Halloran looked impatient. "There's no point. I'm just going to talk to mall security and see if I can't find this guy on one of their cameras."

"In that case, I'm definitely coming with you. I saw a whole lot more than the camera caught so there's a good chance I can make a positive ID."

O'Halloran looked like he wanted to argue, but Jenna didn't give him the chance. Tucking the strap of her handbag over her shoulder, she made a beeline for the mall entrance.

The security office was cramped, and the duty officer, a tall, impressively built Polynesian woman, wasn't happy about letting them in.

O'Halloran flashed his business card and ID.

Jenna started to explain that she had an upcoming book signing in the mall, when the security guard interrupted her with a grin. She knew exactly who Jenna was, because she was halfway through her latest book.

She pulled the book out of her desk drawer and introduced herself as Selene. After a short, animated conversation, Jenna obligingly signed the book.

Selene eyed O'Halloran curiously. "You look familiar, too."

Jenna felt her face warm. She quickly passed the book, front cover down, back to Selene. Now was not a great time for O'Halloran to know that by some weird coincidence, the male model her publisher had used looked uncannily like him.

O'Halloran closed the door on the small office. "You've probably seen me around. I used to be a detective down at Auckland Central."

Selene looked mildly interested. "That's probably it."

Relieved, Jenna let out a breath as Selene sat down at her computer and found the cinema complex cameras.

All six came up on the screen at once. "How far back do you want me to run them?"

O'Halloran checked his watch. "Try an hour, and fast-forward the disks. The guy is balding with glasses and could be carrying a white rose. If we spot him, or anyone carrying a white rose, we can always rewind and go frame by frame—"

"A white rose? Like the one in *Deadly Valentine*?" Selene gave Jenna an outraged look.

Jenna could have hugged her for making the instant connection. It made her own reaction to the rose seem low-key and utterly normal. It was also a warming feeling that someone else could instantly see what the stalker was doing.

O'Halloran's hand landed briefly on the small of Jenna's back, the warmth from his palm burning through the fabric of her suit jacket and distracting her from the conversation, as he moved her closer to the computer screen. He indicated which videos each of them would watch and Jenna tried to concentrate as her two screens began to replay, but her mind was still stubbornly focused on the electrifying moment when O'Halloran had touched her.

The hint had been distinctly possessive and laced with a touch of impatience, because this was all taking a lot longer than he had probably planned, but that didn't change what she had felt.

She recognized what it was, although she hadn't felt it in years—the same riveting, tingling awareness she'd experienced when O'Halloran had stepped into the elevator and said he would be guarding her.

The kind of heart-stopping, searing attraction that had once come close to ruining her life.

As dangerous as this stalker could be, O'Halloran was potentially even more dangerous on a whole other level because she now knew it had taken her years to get over him. In point of fact, she had never gotten over him, because if she had she would have been in another relationship by now.

O'Halloran glanced at her for a heart-pounding moment, making her aware that he had picked up on her restlessness. Mouth suddenly dry, Jenna was more than happy to concentrate on the screen.

Selene frowned as the videos flickered. "If this guy

is using details from your book, then he's got to be a reader, a *fan*."

Still acutely aware of O'Halloran, she kept her gaze glued to the screen. "Men do read my books. I have one male fan who reads every book then emails me."

"Maybe it's him."

"Different email address—"

Selene rolled her eyes. "Don't be fooled by that. He probably has one address to romance you, the other to scare you, know what I mean? You should take this to the police."

Jenna blinked at the connection Selene had made. A connection she hadn't considered, but now realized she should. Although it made her feel faintly sick to think that her favourite fan could be just one side of a psychotic personality. "I've already spoken to the police."

"Huh. In that case I bet they weren't helpful."

O'Halloran's expression was impatient. "Police have to follow procedure. Cyber bullying and internet offences are rife. They can't commit man hours on the strength of an email that contains no specific threat."

Jenna peered at a man who appeared to be skulking behind a group of Japanese tourists. "Apparently you have to be hurt before they take that kind of thing seriously."

"Sounds like exactly what happened with my ex." Selene cast a dark look at the banks of monitors. "That's why I took this job. This way I get to sit and watch the entrances all day. If I see anyone even remotely *resembling* Dean I call ground security. Honey, you should get the cops to run a check on your—" she sketched quotation marks in the air "—*good* fan. Sounds to me like a definite case of Jekyll and Hyde."

She stopped one of the videos, hit a series of keys to zoom in on a bald man, then abandoned the inspection when the zoom revealed that the man was elderly with a moustache. "What's this fan's name?"

"He just calls himself Lydell88."

"That settles it. If he genuinely likes your books, why doesn't he use his full name? Or, for that matter," she muttered darkly, "his *real* name. You don't seriously think anyone today is called Lydell?"

O'Halloran indicated the screen closest to him. "There's our man."

Selene froze the image and zoomed in on a man wearing a brown jacket and a ball cap. Jenna's stomach tightened. The ball cap, aside from hiding any sign of baldness, obscured most of the man's face. He wasn't carrying a rose, but he did have a shopping bag.

Selene started the video playing again. While she and O'Halloran watched the man progress through the mall, she worked with two other screens. The result was that they were able to watch Ball Cap practically until he stepped into the movie theatre.

Selene played the last video through again. All the hairs at Jenna's nape lifted as she watched the calm, methodical progress of the figure, the occasional glint of glasses as his face always angled away from the cameras.

If she hadn't been sure before, she was now. The glasses fit, as did his size and the brown jacket. He seemed younger than she had expected, but maybe that had more to do with her perception that bald men were older, which absolutely was not the case. The clincher was that he had gone to the same movie she had, and arrived there early. It was him.

O'Halloran's expression was remote. "Whoever he is, he seems to know exactly where the cameras are."

Selene nodded. "He keeps his head down, his face away from the camera. I'd say he's done his homework."

Jenna studied the blurred image, which supplied approximate height and build, but little else to add to what they already had. "A shame we can't see the rose, that would have been conclusive."

O'Halloran shrugged. "Farrell wouldn't jump through any hoops even if we could see the rose. The fact is, you can't prove he left it there for you in the first place, because there was no card. Anyone could have gone and sat in the front row and found the rose."

As much as she hated to admit it, Jenna had to agree.

Every piece of "evidence" she had was frustratingly without substance. All she had were a gut feeling and a few details from a fictional book that seemed to be coming true in her own life, none of them particularly menacing or life-threatening. Yet.

O'Halloran produced another business card, scribbled on the back of it and handed it to Selene. "Can you email me a copy of that footage?"

Selene took the card. "No problem. Hey!" She laughed and shook her head. "I know why you're so familiar."

Jenna groaned inwardly as Selene dragged out her copy of *Deadly Valentine* and turned it over on the desk, so the vibrant cover with its larger-than-life, half-naked hero was displayed.

Selene stared at O'Halloran. "You look like Cutler." She looked at the cover then back at O'Halloran again. "Man, that's freaky. You could *be* Cutler."

Chapter 8

O'Halloran insisted they pay a visit to Auckland Central, and take the rose in for fingerprinting.

Jenna slid into the front passenger seat of his truck, which was black and sleek and upholstered with leather. She had decided to leave her little Porsche in the parking lot, since the mall was so close to home. At this time of night it wouldn't be easy finding parking near Auckland Central Police Station.

Farrell wasn't in, but one of O'Halloran's old colleagues took Jenna's statement, and packaged and booked the rose for fingerprinting. A couple of days, max, and they would have a result, provided the perpetrator had a fingerprint record.

By the time they walked back to O'Halloran's car, the sun was setting, and the streets were filled with couples strolling to one of the many restaurants located along Ponsonby Road.

O'Halloran unlocked and held her door. When he climbed behind the wheel, he didn't immediately start the engine. "I don't know about you, but I'm hungry."

Jenna, still on edge since those moments in Selene's office, and the woman's blunt comment that he looked like the hero of *Deadly Valentine*, was so hungry she felt faint. "I could eat something."

"Take-out, or do you want to go to a restaurant?"

"Take-out, please." Then she wouldn't have to look at O'Halloran across a table while they ate and face the unpalatable truth that had hit her in Selene's office. That one of the reasons she had never been able to forget O'Halloran was that she had been unconsciously patterning all of her heroes on him.

He started the car and merged with traffic while they debated what to eat. Because her workday was so sedentary, she needed to watch her weight so, in the end, she opted for Chinese.

After collecting the food, O'Halloran placed the paper sack of containers on the backseat. "We'll pick up your car first."

Minutes later, he turned into the mall parking lot. After checking that no one was lurking around, he waited for her to get in the car then leaned down and spoke through the open window. "I'll follow you."

Her fingers tightened on the wheel. "Where are we going?" Although she had a sneaking suspicion.

"Your place. I was going to check out your house tomorrow, but it's a better idea to have a look around now."

A small chill went down her spine. Until that point

she hadn't known how seriously O'Halloran was taking her allegation of being stalked.

She didn't voice the other thought that had been dominating her mind ever since O'Halloran had asked if the guy in the cinema had approached her.

She had taken his photo. It wasn't a good one, but he didn't know that. She had also taken the rose, which quite possibly had his fingerprints on the wrapping.

Whoever he was, he was more calculating and methodical than the misspelt email he had sent would seem to suggest, which told Jenna that the mistakes in the email had probably been deliberate. A smokescreen created by someone who understood the process of criminal profiling.

And he now had to assume she was in a position to identify him, that she could be a threat to him.

Wearing a pair of overalls branded with the city council logo, and carrying an official-looking clipboard, Branden Tell walked through the block of flats adjacent to Jenna's old mausoleum of a house.

She had taken his photo. He couldn't believe it. *And* she had taken the rose, something else he hadn't anticipated. He didn't know what she had done with it. He had left the mall immediately, just in case she called security, but he had to assume that she had taken the rose to the police.

His fingerprints had to be all over the cellophane, although that wouldn't do Whitmore any good because he didn't have a criminal record.

However, if he did ever get caught on one of the little night excursions he indulged in just to break the boredom, that would change things. The minute the police ran his prints through their computers they would connect him to a whole raft of crimes. They would lock him up and throw away the key. By the time he got out, he would be an old man.

All he had wanted to do was frighten her into withdrawing the book from stores and cancelling the book signings. And if one of the "accidents" he had planned for her worked out, he would send a whole bunch of white roses to the funeral. The last thing he needed was a whole lot of publicity about the book, and people lining up to read *Deadly Valentine*. He didn't think that cops, most of them men, would read Whitmore's books, but *he* had read them so he had to assume that some other men would, too.

After the near miss with the pot plant, he was pretty sure he had her spooked, but she was proving oddly stubborn and resourceful, the complete opposite of the soft, vulnerable Jenna he remembered.

He skimmed the windows of the apartment block, checking for movement or evidence that he was being watched. Although, he expected that at this time of night most residents would be either eating dinner or watching the news on TV.

Jenna living next door to the apartments was a gift because it meant he didn't have to expose himself to an entire street of nosy neighbours by entering through her front gate. Even pretending to repair the gate, he would still attract notice. Most tenants of large apartment blocks were happy to accept the presence of anyone in workman's overalls on the property, automatically assuming they were there on behalf of the landlord.

With a raking glance at the end apartment, which appeared to be empty, he disappeared under the dark overhang of a tree. Tossing the clipboard into the long grass, he levered himself over the wooden fence, landing in the middle of a shaggy green shrub that smelled like insecticide.

Muttering beneath his breath, he worked his way free and emerged from the heavy undergrowth directly opposite a room lined with bookshelves that looked like her office. Walking around to the kitchen, he extracted a set of picks from his pocket. Within seconds, he had the door open.

Taking a penknife from his pocket he released the blade and walked quickly through to Jenna's alarm system, one that a firm he supplied had installed. Accessing the panel, he used the master code to disarm the alarm. He checked his watch. He didn't have much time to find what he needed.

The afternoon light was dimming as he walked through the house. Suppressing his irritation that Jenna had actually gotten wealthy writing those ridiculous books, he found her office and began a systematic search.

Streetlights glowed, illuminating the murky twilight as Marc turned into Jenna's driveway. Her sleek little Porsche disappeared into a garage, so he parked on the broad sweep of gravel fronting an old Victorian house that had had a distinctly modern makeover. The lines of the villa were colonial, but the biscotti paint job with aubergine accents was cutting-edge.

He checked the automatic wrought-iron security gate, frowning a little at the slow-motion action. Someone could easily step through and hide in the shrubbery in the time it took for the gate to close. He would get one of their techs out to reprogram the system. If he had to, he would replace the gate himself.

As he exited the truck, he checked out the front garden, a stretch of smooth lawn edged by a tangle of heavy, dark undergrowth. The border of shrubs was thick enough that it mostly hid the house from the road, but it also provided a convenient hiding place for anyone breaking into the property.

Dark clouds massed overhead. A droplet of rain splashed the bonnet of the truck. The scent of ozone, the quick flight of a bird as if something had disturbed it, combined to set him subtly on edge.

Frowning, he skimmed the street, which was empty. He put his unease down to the incoming electrical storm, which seemed to charge the atmosphere, the cool rush of damp air heightening his senses and making his skin prickle.

He grabbed the sack of take-aways and found his briefcase as Jenna strolled toward him.

The murky light made her creamy skin look magnolia-pale and her eyes even darker. She had unbuttoned her charcoal-grey jacket, revealing the mint-green camisole she was wearing underneath. Silky and utterly feminine, it was a startling contrast to the long grey skirt and red accessories, somehow creating the effect of an edgy, retro elegance that matched the house and garden.

In that moment, Jenna came into sharp focus for Marc.

Her delicate features and stylish haircut aside, there was a strength in her firmly moulded cheekbones, the set of her jaw and the clear direct way she met his gaze. Nine years ago, Jenna hadn't been overtly sexy; the main word that had always sprung to mind had been *nice*. Now her cool, underlying sensuality, which had nothing to do with any descriptive as innocuous as *nice*, hit him like a kick in the chest.

Forcing himself to suppress the kind of reaction he hadn't felt since he was a teenager, he turned his attention back to the garden. "Nice property."

She shrugged. "It's too big, but I've always loved it. I used to walk past it every day on the way to university, and the privacy suits me."

He handed her the paper sack of take-out containers. "Take these inside. I need to do a quick walk around the grounds before it gets too dark. I won't be long."

Her expression tightened fractionally, informing him that she wasn't quite as composed as she seemed. Out of nowhere, like the unscripted moment in the mall parking lot that afternoon, a fierce surge of protectiveness hit him. He had known that the run-in with the stalker had shaken her. He just hadn't realized how much.

Grimly, he clamped down on the impulse to pull her into his arms. He had already pushed the boundaries with the kiss in the elevator; he didn't want to scare Jenna off by pushing for too much, too fast.

He watched the slim, graceful line of Jenna's back as she walked up the steps to the front door, the satiny fall of dark hair shot through with lighter streaks. The attraction that had flared to life when he had met Jenna at the gravesite was showing no signs of fading, and now he didn't expect it to.

He knew his nature. When it came to women, for him the situation had always been black and white. He either felt something or he didn't; there had never been any middle ground.

That was one of the reasons it had been so easy for

him to remain single since Natalie had died. He simply hadn't felt anything strong enough to tempt him into an actual relationship. He'd had occasional casual liaisons, but as convenient as it would have been for those liaisons to grow into something more, a part of him had remained remote and uninvolved.

Until now.

Grimly he registered the growing tension in his body, his utter masculine focus on Jenna.

Jenna turned and shot him a veiled look as she unlocked the door, letting him know in a subtle, entirely feminine way that she had noted his interest but that the jury was still out. "I'll get you a flashlight."

Marc's gaze shuttered. "There's no need, I have one in the truck." And the last thing he wanted was for Jenna to insist on coming with him, just in case he found evidence that someone *had* been on the property.

He checked to make sure Jenna had disappeared inside then collected the flashlight and the other piece of equipment he wanted: a Glock 17 handgun with a shoulder holster.

Shrugging out of his jacket, he pulled on the shoulder holster, fastened the webbing then unlocked the metal storage case, which held the gun. With swift, practiced movements, he slotted the magazine into its casing, holstered the gun and shrugged back into his jacket.

Picking up the flashlight, he locked the truck and began a systematic examination of the fence and garden.

In the thickening twilight, the powerful beam had the effect of making the evening seem darker than it was. Sounds seemed more distinct, the scents of city and garden intensified. He waded through foliage, checking the fenceline, and looking for areas of crushed foliage. A few steps farther on and he discovered a dilapidated shed.

Directing the beam of the flashlight into the shed, which was filled with a jumble of old tools and firewood, he kept moving. Another few steps and he found a damaged shrub and trampled ground directly across from a room with a large bay window and a desk. At a guess, Jenna's office.

From the kitchen window, Jenna glimpsed the flickering beam of the flashlight and the pale flash of O'Halloran's shirt as she placed the take-out containers in the oven. O'Halloran had taken a good five minutes to work his way around one side of the house, she guessed it would take him the same to check out the other side, and in the meantime she didn't want their food to go cold.

Tiny droplets of rain speckled the window. She flicked on a light to brighten up the kitchen, and frowned when nothing happened. She tried a second light switch with no better luck. Power outages weren't uncommon, especially in her suburb with its old plantings of graceful but tall trees. Every time they got a strong wind, branches swayed and hit lines, or came down altogether.

Shrugging, she hunted out candles and a lighter and laid them on the table where they'd be easy to find then strolled toward the stairs, intending to change into some warmer clothing before O'Halloran came in.

She flicked on another light switch, just in case the problem in the kitchen was a blown fuse and the rest of the house still had power. When the hall remained dim, she frowned. The weather was definitely deteriorating, but as yet the wind was hardly strong enough to cause a problem.

A small trickle of unease, courtesy of the creepy episode in the mall, inched down her spine. Although it was ridiculous to think that anyone could have been in the house. The power had been on when she'd walked into her home, because she had turned off the alarm when she'd walked into the hall.

Added to that, the alarm included a wireless connection to her broadband modem. If anyone tried to interfere with the alarm in any way, aside from the ear-splitting siren and instant call to the security company, it was programmed to text her phone with a message. If anyone had broken into the house, she would have known about it before she had gotten home.

Still feeling vaguely unsettled but putting it down to the crazy day and the fact that she was hungry, she walked through the shadowy interior of the house, her heels echoing on polished floorboards. Movement caught her eye. Her pulse jumped, but it was only O'Halloran glimpsed through one of the French doors in the sitting room, checking the fence.

Letting out a breath, she forced herself to relax. O'Halloran was large, muscled and an ex-cop who had been a decorated member of the Special Tactics Squad, an elite frontline squad of armed police. If her poisonous fan was anywhere near the property, then he was the one who had the problem.

On impulse, she walked through to her office and checked her laptop. The battery should have kept it going, and she had a surge protector, but sometimes freak occurrences like lightning strikes could fry the electrics anyway.

She glimpsed O'Halloran again. He lifted a hand. Reassured by his presence, but still on edge, she disconnected the laptop from the power source and, on impulse, decided to take it upstairs. It had about four hours of battery, so if she wasn't too tired later on, she could work at the small portable desk in her bedroom.

Still feeling oddly tense, she walked upstairs, deposited the laptop on the portable desk positioned in one corner of her room and kicked off her heels. She quickly changed into slim-fitting jeans and a polo-necked midnight-blue sweater that clung softly to her hips.

With the light almost completely gone now, she searched in her bedside table and found a penlight.

She glimpsed O'Halloran out of her bedroom window as she slipped into more comfortable flats and her breath lodged in her throat as she recalled the tension that had gripped her as she had unlocked the front door.

O'Halloran's gaze had been focused and intent. In her various dating forays she had glimpsed desire, and quite often liking, but none of her dates had ever looked at her in quite *that* way.

Somewhere downstairs a floorboard creaked, pulling her out of her reverie. She could no longer see O'Halloran outside. Frowning, she walked out onto the landing and stared into the deep well of shadow cast by the staircase.

The house was old. It creaked when the timbers warmed up during the day, then again when it cooled down at night. There was nothing to be alarmed about, but with the fading light, and without her cheerful array of lamps glowing, the atmosphere was definitely creepy.

She should flick on the penlight and walk down the

stairs, but some preternatural instinct kept her frozen in place in the dark, her gaze glued to the hall below. Despite O'Halloran's presence, she kept getting an unnerving tingling sensation down her spine.

It was stress, she reassured herself. With the unpleasant incident at the cinema and two interviews at Auckland Central, it had not been an easy day.

Another creak, as if someone was stepping lightly, sent adrenaline shooting through her veins.

Someone was there. "O'Halloran?"

Chapter 9

Mood grim, O'Halloran completed the circuit of the house, ending up back by the area of trampled shrubbery. The weather was closing in, with heavy, dark clouds massing. Fat droplets of rain splashed down as he passed the beam of the flashlight over the trampled area.

Something pale gleamed in amongst the shrubbery.

All the small hairs at Marc's nape lifted. A piece of cloth, or paper, that hadn't been there five minutes ago. He said something short and hard beneath his breath. He must be losing his edge.

The cold itch down his spine now made sense, because whoever had broken the shrub had been on the property while he searched it.

Flicking the flashlight off, he levered himself up and smoothly over the fence.

Bare minutes later, as he checked the vehicles parked

out on the street, the niggling sense that something was wrong coalesced into cold knowledge.

He flicked a glance at the still darkened house and began to run, cutting back through the property with its ranks of apartments. When they had driven in to Jenna's drive, the electronically controlled front gate had worked and he had noticed a porch light glowing. In the past few minutes, with the fading sun, Jenna should have switched on lights. The big old house should be clearly visible from the street. Instead it was shrouded in darkness.

When he had done his last circuit of the house, he hadn't noticed the porch light glowing. Either Jenna had switched it off, which didn't make sense, or in the minutes since they had arrived, the power to the house had been cut.

The intruder hadn't left, and he wasn't outside.

He was *in* the house.

Chills running down her spine, Jenna padded out onto the landing.

In the time she had been upstairs, the last light had gone. The glow of sodium streetlamps flowed in the front windows, hammering home the fact that her power outage was an isolated event.

She didn't know how it had happened, but she had to assume that someone had gotten inside the house and switched the power off. Her jaw tightened. The first thing she should have done was walk out to the front hall and check the fuse box, but she had been so distracted by O'Halloran's presence that she hadn't thought to check.

She paused, holding her breath for long seconds as

she listened and allowed her eyes to adjust to the heavy gloom.

A scraping sound from the direction of her office made her stiffen.

It couldn't be O'Halloran, he was still outside. She had seen him just minutes ago strolling toward the left side of the house. If he had entered by the front door, with its steps and hardwood verandah, regardless of how light he was on his feet, she would have heard him.

The flicker of a shadow made her heart slam in her chest. A flowing solid shape, darker than the pooling shadows below, emerged from her office and paused at the base of the stairs.

Suddenly the tension that had hit her when she had collected her laptop made sense. The intruder hadn't just been in the house, *he had been in her office when she had collected her laptop.*

If he was in her office, it also followed that he had probably been after her laptop, because there wasn't much else of value in there.

She sensed more than saw him looking up the staircase, and froze. She was not directly in his line of sight. She was standing off to one side. With most of the bedroom doors shut, closing out any ambient light flowing through windows, this part of the house was now in almost complete darkness. As exposed as she felt, the odds were that he couldn't see her.

Another creak sent another small nervy shock of adrenaline through her. That was the second-to-bottom tread, which meant he was now on the staircase, and climbing.

If it was the guy who had been stalking her, she had to assume it was because he wanted the laptop.

Although she wasn't sure what he thought he would achieve by stealing her computer. The only possible reason would be to hurt her by depriving her of her work and sabotaging the publication of her next two books.

She considered her options. She could yell for O'Halloran and hope that would scare away the intruder. But given that he had to know O'Halloran was on the property, and that he had chosen to remain in the house despite the danger, she couldn't bank on that option.

He also wanted her laptop badly enough to come upstairs, knowing that she was here. Possibly the only thing she could do was stop him from taking her computer.

She had done a self-defence course, and she kept in good shape jogging and working out. He no doubt thought that taking the laptop off her was going to be easy, but after the day she'd had, if he wanted it, she decided grimly, he was going to have to rip it out of her cold, dead hands.

Easing her feet out of her shoes, Jenna backed away from the landing rail and the slow, gliding advance of the intruder. The back of one hand brushed against the wall.

Swallowing the sudden tightening panic that gripped her chest, her throat, she followed the wall until she hit the frame of her door. Her room was lighter than the landing, although just enough that she could make out the silvery gleam of her laptop.

Sliding the penlight into her jeans pocket, she picked up the computer and shoved it under her mattress then looked around a little wildly. In the end, out of time, she picked up a heavy earthenware vase that was sitting on one of her dressers and positioned herself to one side of the door. If she could hit him hard on the head, with any luck, he would go down. Then she could run. It wasn't much of a plan, but it was all she had.

Holding the vase above her head, she stared hard at the opening. The quality of light in the doorway altered. She hadn't heard anything and, eerily, she still couldn't see anything until he turned his head and the frail light flowing through the window gleamed on pale irises. It was then she realized the reason she couldn't see him was that he was dressed entirely in black, and he was wearing a balaclava.

The urn came down with a thud that sent a shock-wave up both her arms. He grunted, but in the instant before the vase hit his head, he had shifted sideways and it had bounced off his shoulder.

The sound of the vase shattering split the air. "Bitch."

A gloved hand clamped her throat and she was shoved back against the wall with force. The back of her head connected sharply. Convulsively, she reached for breath, but his fingers squeezed, cutting off air.

Above the pounding of blood in her ears, the la-boured rasp of his breathing, dimly, Jenna regis-tered a thundering sound. Not the approaching storm. O'Halloran was coming up the stairs.

The explosive sound of something shattering, fol-lowed by a sharp crack had sent a kick of adrenaline through Marc that almost stopped his heart.

Grimly castigating himself for not considering that Jenna's stalker could still be on the property after he'd noted the crushed foliage, he lunged up the last two stairs. The Glock clasped in his hands, he crossed the landing and stepped into a room filled with cold swirling air.

For a split second he thought he was too late, then his eyes, by now adjusted to the darkness, easily picked out Jenna sitting on the floor, gasping for breath, and a curtain flapping in the breeze.

Before he could ask if she was all right, her gaze sliced to his, steady and oddly fierce. She stabbed a finger at the window. "I'm okay. He went off the balcony."

Marc didn't stop to ask why her voice was so raspy. By the sounds he had heard it was a given that she had been hurt. From the shards of crockery crunching underfoot, he savagely hoped she had given as good as she'd got.

Jaw tight, he holstered the Glock and flowed out onto the balcony and over the side. As he climbed down the gnarled limbs of wisteria that clung to the house and festooned the balcony, he made a mental note that the ornamental shrub had to go. If it could be climbed down, that meant someone could also use it to gain entrance to the house.

A crashing sound below, at a guess the plastic waste disposal bin he'd seen tucked discreetly outside the laundry being knocked over, signalled that the intruder was down.

Marc hit the ground running. He glimpsed a flickering movement and registered that the reason he was finding it so hard to pinpoint the intruder was because he was dressed entirely in black, including a balaclava.

Cursing himself for not having a pair of night-vision goggles on hand, he waded through undergrowth. From now on he would make sure he had the full kit for night surveillance stored in the trunk of his car at all times.

Flinging aside whippy branches, he boosted himself up and over the fence, but, from the sound of pounding footsteps, he knew he was going to be too late. He ran out on the road in time to see a pair of taillights winking as a van turned and accelerated away.

Sucking in a deep breath, he turned to study the property he had just run through. The intruder had been unexpectedly smart. He had bypassed the expensive properties on the other two boundaries, and the street entrance, in favor of using one that had multiple tenants. Judging from the bikes stacked against walls, the old sofas and boxes of empty beer cans, most of them were students. World War Three could break out in their front yard and they wouldn't notice.

He wouldn't underestimate the stalker again. Although he hadn't been caught entirely flatfooted. He had bagged the clipboard and pen he had found lying in the grass.

More importantly, he had gotten the registration number for the van.

Chills running up and down her spine, Jenna stared out into the storm-tossed night and watched as O'Halloran climbed over her fence with fluid ease.

That was too easy, she thought starkly. She was going to have to build the fence higher. Stepping back inside her bedroom, she remembered the penlight in her pocket, extracted it and flicked on the reassuring beam of light.

Hands shaking with an overload of adrenaline and reaction, she closed the French doors and locked them then turned to survey the mess. Pottery shards littered the floor and somehow the dresser nearest the door had been overturned, probably when the intruder had stumbled off balance after she'd hit him. A set of elegant glass perfume bottles were scattered amongst the pottery shards, some of them also smashed.

Stepping out onto the landing, she made her way gingerly downstairs. Her head was throbbing from the crack she'd received when the back of her head had hit the wall, and her throat felt tender. She hadn't looked, but she was guessing she would have a necklace of interesting bruises by morning. She also felt a little weird, unsettled and shaky, her pulse pounding way too fast. Mild shock, she realized.

A shudder went through her when she remembered the moment her assailant had gripped her throat. The hold had been tight, and more than a little personal. In that moment, with his eyes glittering into hers, she had gotten the distinct impression that whoever he was, he hated her.

If he hated her, it followed he had to know her.

Swallowing painfully, she reached the hall just as O'Halloran strode in the front door.

His gaze locked on hers, and she drew a swift breath.

His expression was remote, implacable, his eyes shooting cold fire.

"Are you all right?"

"Yes."

"You don't look it."

"Thanks," she said shakily.

A split second later, she was in his arms, his hold firm enough that she could feel the unmistakable bulge of a shoulder holster.

She remembered O'Halloran stepping through her bedroom door, a large black gun held in both hands, his toneless voice, the efficient way he had checked on her before ghosting out onto the balcony and over the side. She had heard the intruder clambering down her wisteria vine; O'Halloran had made almost no noise, he'd seemed to move in a bubble of silence.

As if sensing her tension, O'Halloran eased her a little closer, and wrapped her tighter, cradling her against his chest. His warm palm cupped her nape, urging her to rest her head on his shoulder.

"Ouch."

His fingers probed and found the bump forming at the back of her head. "He hit you."

She blinked at the utter lack of emotion in his voice and then, like a bolt out of the blue, she finally got it, she finally got *him*. O'Halloran wasn't either emotionless or disconnected; he was blazing mad.

Some people got emotional in stressful situations. From what she knew of O'Halloran, he never did, which was what had made him such a good cop and the perfect bodyguard.

She couldn't remember one single occasion, even counting the tragic house fire, when he had lost control. Nine years ago, when she had broken up with him, had been a case in point. His calm, measured response had convinced her she had done the right thing.

She had always thought his lack of response had signalled a basic inability to feel, but she was suddenly, stunningly aware that the opposite was the case. O'Halloran cared; the measured response and flat voice was just his way of coping.

"He didn't exactly hit me," she said cautiously. "My head bounced off the wall."

There was a moment of tense silence. "What else?"

For a brief moment, she simply soaked in the careful way he was cradling her, the knowledge that O'Halloran cared that she had been hurt. "Just the bruising on my throat."

O'Halloran swore softly. "I need some light."

Releasing her, he gently prised the tiny penlight from her hand, walked the few steps to the fuse box and beamed the light into the cavity while he turned the power back on.

He flicked a switch and the hall flooded with light. Peeling back the polo-neck of her sweater, he gently touched the tender area, sending streamers of tingling heat radiating out from that one small point of contact. "I'm going to kill him."

The soft flat statement was subtly claiming and wholly electrifying. Although, Jenna knew she shouldn't build too much into it. She had just been threatened and attacked, and O'Halloran was with her in the role of protector. He was male, powerful and in control in the kind of take-charge, alpha way that was hard to resist, but she also knew that he would fiercely guard whoever was in his care.

He handed her the flashlight then insisted on examining the bump on the back of her head.

She winced as he probed, but when he asked if she wanted a doctor, she refused. "I'm not concussed. I had concussion when I was a kid and I know what that feels like. That's just sissy bruising."

O'Halloran's mouth kicked up at the corners. The glint of humour, the moment of uncomplicated intimacy, filled her with a crazy, giddy warmth.

After everything she had been through that day, Jenna reflected, the most important thing shouldn't be that somehow, despite all of the bad things that had happened, she and O'Halloran were in it together.

O'Halloran insisted that she walk through to the kitchen and sit down while he got ice for her head. He turned on lights, found a bag of frozen peas, wrapped a kitchen towel around it and made her hold it against the bump.

He opened cupboards. "Where do you keep your first-aid supplies?"

She directed him to the pantry then obediently swallowed the painkillers he gave her along with a glass of water.

She insisted he also hand her a second ice pack for her neck, this one frozen beans. When he frowned at the request, she gave him a level look. "If ice can take down the bruising on my head, it can do the same job on my neck. Since I've got a book launch to attend tomorrow evening, it would be kind of nice not to look like someone just tried to strangle me."

Especially when photos would be taken that would appear in local newspapers and on various internet sites. The last thing she wanted was to give her poisonous fan the satisfaction of knowing that he had hurt her.

Luckily, her sweater had cushioned her neck and make-up would hide some of the marks, but if the bruising was too profound, the dark colour would still show through.

While she held the two packs of frozen vegetables in place, O'Halloran made calls, one to Auckland Central, one to McCabe. When he hung up, his expression was grim. "The police are sending someone out. He should be here in the next fifteen minutes."

O'Halloran relieved her of the job of holding the peas

at the back of her head. "Now tell me everything that happened from the time you walked inside."

As emotionlessly as possible, Jenna related the sequence of events. Going back over what had happened kept sending small shocks of adrenaline through her and she felt furious and shaky in turns. It was an interesting effect.

O'Halloran said something soft under his breath. "Honey, I'm sorry, but this has to be done. When the detective gets here, he's going to ask you the same questions. If we go over it now, it'll be easier when you have to give a statement."

"This is my problem." Jenna held out one hand. Despite her efforts she couldn't keep it steady.

O'Halloran grinned quick and hard. "I've got an idea that might help. Where do you keep your liquor?"

"There's brandy and sherry in the pantry."

He opened the pantry door and took down a bottle. "Which do you prefer?"

"Neither," she muttered flatly. "I use them for cooking."

"Too bad." She heard the click of a glass tumbler, the sound of pouring, and placed a bet with herself that he had chosen the brandy.

She was wrong, he had quarter-filled the glass with sherry.

"It's got 'fortified' on the label," he said dryly, "there's more sugar. That's key, so drink up."

"Is that an order?" With a grimace, she sipped. The rich, syrupy flavour spread across her tongue and flowed like liquid fire down her throat.

He replaced the cap on the bottle. "Last I heard women don't take orders anymore."

Jenna choked then had to cough. She hastily placed the glass on the table before she spilled the sherry. O'Halloran was being downright charming, but he wasn't flirting with her. He was just trying to help her past her little battle with shock.

He gave her a gentle thump on the back. "Better?"

She gave a hiccoughing gulp then drew a long breath. "*Distracted* is more the word."

"Good. I've got another remedy." Removing the bag of frozen beans from her neck, he tossed it on the table and hooked out a chair.

Moments later, he scooped her off her chair and sat down with her on his lap.

Chapter 10

Too surprised to protest, Jenna grabbed at his shoulders to steady herself. "I haven't heard of this remedy." The muscular hardness of his thighs beneath hers and the furnace heat of his chest and arms were not exactly comforting, but he had definitely driven out the shaky chills and given her something else to obsess about.

One big hand curled around her nape, pressing her head against his shoulder. "It's not textbook."

She inhaled O'Halloran's warmth and scent. Okay, now he was definitely flirting with her, but the rumble of his voice, the steady pound of his heart, was soothing. She gave up the idea of bolting and stayed in place. "I could use another drink."

He pressed the tumbler of sherry into her hands and waited until she drank. "Can you remember if he said anything?"

A flashback of the black balaclava and the pale glint of his eyes made her stiffen. She couldn't prevent the small shudder that went through her.

"Have another sip, it'll help."

Obediently, she took another mouthful of sherry, then a second, waited for the warming effect, then tried to think. "Other than a nasty name, nothing. The only thing I really noticed was that he was angry. Make that very angry, and it was personal."

Her stomach tightened at the thought that someone in her past hated her enough to break into her home, *wait there while she was in the house*, then attack her, even knowing O'Halloran was outside. "I must know him. When I looked into his eyes…" She frowned, trying to catch an elusive wisp of memory.

"We can work through that later. What else did you notice? The colour of his skin, the way he talked, the way he smelled."

She closed her eyes. The instant she did that, O'Halloran's heartbeat seemed louder. She forced herself to relax, concentrating on the soothing regular beat, the cosy encircling warmth of his arms.

Taking a breath, she deliberately visualised the moment she had stood in the doorway, poised to hit the stalker with the vase. She tensed as she recalled the blackness filling the doorway then the shock of realisation when she had seen the glint of his eyes. "European. He had light skin and eyes. He was tall, because I had to look up, but not as tall as you. Maybe about six-one."

She thought back and remembered one other detail. "He smelled like new appliances. When I bought a new dishwasher and washing machine for the house and unpacked them, it was that smell. The polystyrene packing, I guess."

"That gels with the vehicle he used to make his getaway. It was an appliance van."

She straightened and stared into O'Halloran's eyes. "You got the number."

His mouth kicked up at the corners in that mesmerising way. "I got the number."

A dizzying sense of triumph and satisfaction spiralled through her. As scary as the stalker was, she thought, he wasn't nearly as scary as O'Halloran. She had wondered what had been taking O'Halloran so long; now she had her answer. He had been busy outsmarting her stalker.

His gaze locked with hers. "Honey, I'm sorry I took so long to get to you. When I realized the house was in darkness, I almost had a heart attack. I knew he had to be inside."

Grimly she concentrated on the amber colour of the sherry. Unfortunately, the adrenaline-laced flashback to the moment his hand had clamped onto her throat was hard to stop. "He must have been inside already when we drove in. I didn't realize until I was upstairs. I think he was after my laptop."

His gaze sharpened. "Did he get it?"

"No way. I hid it under the mattress."

"Then you hit him with the vase." He grinned. "That's my girl."

Jenna tried to squash the burst of pure pleasure that glowed through her at the statement. Despite the fact that she was sitting on his lap, she was not by any stretch of the imagination "his girl." If she wanted to underline that fact all she had to do was recall that O'Halloran hadn't wanted to guard her and had done his best to fob her off on someone else. "I was going for his head. Unfortunately I got his shoulder instead."

The faint shaking of O'Halloran's chest alerted her to the fact that he was laughing.

Jenna blinked and tried to look away from the mesmerising glint of white teeth, the sudden glimpse of the carefree, younger O'Halloran she had once known, but the sherry had kicked in and she was feeling just the tiniest bit woozy.

Feeling suddenly, ridiculously self-conscious she relaxed back against his chest and tried not to love it when his arms tightened around her. "This could get to be addictive."

"Not as addictive as this."

Cupping her chin, he gently angled her head. "I'm going to kiss you. If you don't want it, just say so and I won't."

Her heart slammed once, hard. She found herself caught in the net of his dark gaze, riveted by the mouthwatering cut of his cheekbones and the sexy hollows beneath, riveted by his mouth. The fact that he had given her a choice, putting her in the driving seat with the kiss, was seductive in itself, and was more than a little manipulative, she decided. But even knowing that O'Halloran was managing her in a distinctly male way, just the fact that he *wanted* to do so had the effect of draining away any objection.

And she should have an objection. Over the past few minutes, O'Halloran had moved in on her in stages, holding her, caring for her injuries, sitting her on his lap. Allowing more was tantamount to giving permission for sex.

He lowered his head, his breath washed over her

cheek and, in that moment, Jenna knew she wasn't going to move, and she wasn't going to say no.

She was twenty-nine, and since O'Halloran, she had never been able to choose anyone else. She had never been able to even relax with any of the men she had dated, or enjoy being kissed, which had ruled out intimate touching and sex.

She'd been accused of being frigid, but she knew that wasn't the case. She wanted to fall in love. She wanted the dizzying highs and the gritty lows, the laughter and the tears and the tender moments, and she definitely wanted the sex.

She wanted to touch and taste and smell; she wanted the earthy, no-holds-barred intimacy of being naked with her man while he made love to her.

Dispassionately, she stared at the hard line of O'Halloran's jaw, the sexy five o'clock shadow. Her problem was that O'Halloran had spoiled her for anyone else. As hard as she tried not to, every time she met someone new, unconsciously, she compared him to O'Halloran.

Cupping his jaw with her free hand, she lifted up the last few inches and touched her mouth to his. She felt his surprise, the hitch in his breath. A split second later, O'Halloran's arms closed more tightly around her, although he kept the kiss soft, giving her the opportunity to draw back if she wanted.

A pastiche of conflicting emotions threw her back to the intense moments in the elevator, then further back still, nine years, to the incandescent lovemaking in his apartment.

Heat shimmered and pooled. Memories, new and old,

seemed to shift and meld as she wound her arms around O'Halloran's neck and gave herself over to the kiss.

His palm flattened in the center of her back, the heat of it burning through her sweater as he urged her closer. Her breasts were flattened against the hard wall of his chest, her nipples pebble-hard. The firm shape of his arousal against one thigh sent a sharp, hot pang through her.

Dimly she noted that it was time to stop, climb out of O'Halloran's lap and regain some semblance of control. But with O'Halloran still holding her with seducing firmness while his mouth settled more heavily on hers, stopping was rapidly becoming an abstract concept.

He lifted his head, his gaze narrowed and glittering, as if he'd divined her intention to stop. In that moment, Jenna realized that the concept of experimenting with O'Halloran was inherently, dangerously flawed.

She felt as if she'd been kicked in the stomach. She hadn't ever been able to forget O'Halloran for one very good reason. Nine years ago she hadn't just been attracted to him; she had fallen in love.

That was why it had been so difficult seeing O'Halloran and Natalie as a married couple, and why she had kept a careful distance.

The enormity of the mistake she'd made in falling for O'Halloran made her stomach hollow out. She should have met someone in a safe, steady, "normal" job. A man she could have settled down with and started a family.

To make matters worse, if anything, she was even more attracted to this older, grimmer version of O'Halloran.

O'Halloran reclaimed her lips and all of the reasons

she should pull back evaporated on a raw surge of heat. Instead, she cupped his face and kissed him back, wallowing in the scent and taste of him, his hard, masculine warmth.

O'Halloran hadn't come near her in years, now, within days of that meeting in the cemetery, he was making no bones about wanting her. And crazily, she was teetering on the brink of going to bed with him.

A vibrating pulse resonated through the kitchen.

O'Halloran lifted his head. "I need to answer that."

Calmly, he reached around her and retrieved the phone from the kitchen table, while keeping her on his lap, and answered the call.

The abrupt change from passion to calm neutrality, while O'Halloran fielded the call, was like a dash of cold water.

Not prepared to sit tamely on his lap while he talked business, Jenna unlooped her arms from around his neck and eased off his lap. Not quite saved by the bell, but close. She had forgotten O'Halloran's knack of switching from hot to cold. That macho, distinctly alpha quality had confused her in the past, but she was not prepared to be confused now.

Grabbing the rapidly thawing bags of frozen vegetables, she replaced them in the freezer then remembered to check the take-aways.

As soon as she opened the oven door and smelled the aroma of spicy Chinese, her stomach rumbled. Probably the reason she felt so shaky was that she needed to eat.

"Let me help you with that."

Jenna noted O'Halloran's watchful gaze, as if he was assessing her mood and had judged correctly that she had backed off. "If you want to help you can set the table. The plates are in the cupboard next to the pantry."

She grabbed an oven mitt and set warm containers of food on the kitchen counter, breathing a sigh of relief as O'Halloran began setting out cutlery and plates.

The intercom at the front door buzzed, indicating that someone was at the front gate.

Jenna's head came up sharply enough to send a throb of pain through her skull.

"I'll get it." O'Halloran's gaze was still oddly neutral, his voice deep and flat. "That'll be either Hansen or McCabe."

A small shudder of reaction went through her as he strode out of the kitchen to see who was out on the street. She was jumpy, but then a lot had happened in the space of the past forty or so minutes.

Leaning back against the counter, she felt the lump at the back of her head. Thankfully, it had responded to the ice and had mostly flattened out.

Although, that wasn't her only problem.

She touched lips that still tingled and burned from O'Halloran's kiss. After nine bland, benign years without any discernible emotional highs or lows, the past had come back and bitten her, with a vengeance.

She was still trying to figure out just where the biggest danger lay: from the masked intruder she had upset with her latest book, or the ex-boyfriend she had hired to protect her.

Marc stepped out into the rain and disengaged the manual lock for the front gate, allowing a sleek, black four-wheel drive to glide into a space beside his truck. He wasn't surprised to see McCabe step out because

the SUV was his. What he hadn't expected was for Mc-
Cabe to bring company in the form of Carter Rawlings
and Gabriel West. Both former Special Air Service as-
sociates of McCabe's, Marc had met them a few years
back during a dangerous situation that had developed
when he had been staying in Carter's hometown, Jackson's Ridge.

Since then they had gotten into the habit of socialising on a regular basis. Marc had even found himself
nominated for duty as a godparent for Carter's first
child, a little hellion called Blake. Saying yes had been
a tough moment, but Carter hadn't brooked a refusal.
He had understood how much Marc had lost.

Marc lifted a brow at their evening clothes. "Looks
like I interrupted something."

McCabe shrugged out of his jacket, jerked loose the
knot of his tie and tossed both in the rear passenger seat.
"We were at an SAS reunion dinner."

"More like a wake if you ask me." Carter, who had
probably gotten rid of the jacket and tie at the beginning of the evening, walked around the bonnet of the
SUV and clapped Marc on the shoulder. "Sadly, I didn't
recognize anyone."

McCabe frowned. "I saw you talking to Oz."

"That wasn't Oz," Carter said flatly. "Oz had crazy
eyes. Whoever was impersonating him looked—"

"Normal?" The third passenger, Gabriel West, by far
the quietest of the three and, Marc had always thought
privately, the most lethal, stepped just short of the light
flowing from the porch. "You're right. No way was that
the Oz we once knew. He was carrying an extra twenty
pounds and driving a people carrier. I'm going with the
alien abduction scenario."

Carter looked irritable. "He was bald, not green."

West shrugged and extended a hand to Marc. "Whatever. There was no pizza or beer at the reunion, so an executive decision was made."

Marc accepted West's brief handshake, automatically noting the way both McCabe and Rawlings had fanned out slightly. Even though the positioning was probably unintentional, designed to cover arcs of attack, it emphasised that, the banter aside, this was not a social visit.

He had requested backup and McCabe had brought it. All three had once been part of a tight and very successful SAS team. The tendency to fall into the natural rhythms and patterns of a patrol was probably as instinctive and natural to each of them as breathing.

He jerked his head in the direction of the house. "If you're hungry, there are Chinese take-aways in the kitchen."

The door opened, and porch light flared over Jenna, highlighting her delicate curves, the exotic slant of her cheekbones and dark eyes. Three sets of male eyes swivelled. Marc logged the small silence that followed, the automatic aura of male appreciation.

Jenna smiled coolly. "I take it this is the cavalry."

Marc stepped toward Jenna, the move instinctive, blatantly laying claim, he realized. If any of the three men wanted to shake hands they would have to get past him first.

He made introductions and watched over the brief exchanges as Jenna invited them into the house. Even knowing that McCabe, Rawlings and West were all happily married to women they were in love with didn't make any difference. They were competition, and Jenna was single and available.

Until about five minutes ago.

The decision he had made when he had picked up Jenna, sat her in his lap and kissed her, settled in more firmly. He had wanted to comfort her. He had wanted her, period. He didn't know where this would take them long-term, but he had his confirmation that Jenna wanted him.

Marc's jaw tightened at the careful way Jenna avoided his gaze. Now that he had made his decision, he was impatient to claim her, but he was aware that if he pushed too hard he could lose her.

Jenna's reserve had always been about protection, not frigidity. Nine years ago the reason he hadn't been able to reach beyond her reserve was that not only had she lost her father to the military, she had also lost a fiancé.

The situation had been frustrating, but at least he had finally understood why she'd been so wary of him. In retrospect, because he was a cop, it had been a small miracle that she had even consented to go out with him at all.

Discovering that Jenna had been a virgin when they had made love had been a watershed moment. The relationship had ended, but despite the passage of years he had continued to feel proprietorial about her. In a purely masculine sense, she had belonged to him.

Since then she would have had lovers.

Years had passed, and Jenna was single and gorgeous; he had to accept that fact, even if he didn't like it.

He watched as Carter, West and McCabe filed inside as meekly as if butter wouldn't melt in their mouths, when the reality was somewhat different.

Marc had heard some of the stories and read edited Reuters reports of a couple of the SAS missions they had been involved in overseas. They were his friends and no longer in the SAS, but that didn't change the fact that they had been, and still were, should the occasion demand it, bona fide predators.

Jaw tight, he followed them inside the house. McCabe, Rawlings and West wouldn't touch Jenna, but in that moment he logged a salient fact. The world was filled with men who would, in a heartbeat. If he left the way clear for them.

Over his dead body.

Chapter 11

Jenna saw a second vehicle arrive just as O'Halloran was about to close the front door. Her stomach dropped a little as she recognized Elaine Farrell with Detective Hansen.

She activated the gate to let them in the drive and stepped out onto the porch as O'Halloran shook Hansen's hand.

She had told them the intruder had been wearing gloves, so there was no fingerprint evidence to be collected. O'Halloran gave them the licence tag and description of the van.

Twenty minutes later, after giving her statement and having Hansen and Farrell check out her upstairs bedroom, they walked the property in the light, persistent drizzle that had set in, then left.

Jenna had insisted on accompanying O'Halloran and

the two police officers. She had needed to see where the intruder had gotten in, so she could make plans to make the fence secure.

A chill shot down her spine when she saw that the entry point was right across from her office window. Even if the stalker hadn't climbed over the fence, he had probably been able to watch her from the other side.

Wet hair trailing down her back, Jenna stepped into the light and warmth of the entrance hall. O'Halloran, his hair wet and his shirt clinging to broad shoulders, because he had walked through soaking foliage, glided in behind her.

Jenna grabbed towels from the downstairs linen cupboard, kept one for herself and handed the other to O'Halloran. As she strolled back into the kitchen, McCabe, West and Carter stepped in her back door. She saw that they were also wet. They had also been outside. They had obviously been checking out her property although she hadn't seen or heard them.

She collected more towels and handed them out.

Bemused, Jenna listened to the tales bandied back and forth about past operations. A lethal jewel thief who had tried to kill West's wife, Tyler, and the misplaced bullet that had ended West's reputation as untouchable in battle. The saga of the escaped ostriches in Carter's hometown of Jackson's Ridge.

The conversation switched to speculation about her stalker and possible avenues the investigation would take.

McCabe folded his towel when he'd finished with it and placed it neatly on the end of her counter. "If Farrell's got the case, this guy may as well give up now. The lady's got a reputation."

Carter folded his arms over his chest and leaned against the kitchen counter. "Farrell's a gunslinger. No sense of humour, though. The only time I ever saw her smile was when West got shot in the ass—"

A bunched-up towel hit Carter in the midriff.

When he spoke, West's voice was mild. "Do we have to talk about that?"

O'Halloran, who looked as if he was having trouble controlling his mirth, rubbed a hand over his mouth. "Pretty sure Farrell did a lot more than smile. I heard she used her phone camera."

Carter used the towel to blot his hair again then dropped it over the back of a chair. "She used it. I erased the evidence. She made the mistake of putting the phone down while she was booking some guy." He patted West on the shoulder. "You owe me, big-time."

West shot Jenna an embarrassed look. "Ignore them. I was protecting my wife."

McCabe, who had been talking into his cell out in the hall, stepped back into the kitchen. "And we all love it that you went to that extreme."

O'Halloran grinned. "All in the line of duty, and anything beats herding ostriches. I've still got *those* scars."

Jenna discreetly checked on the food in the oven. There wasn't enough for five, so she grabbed fresh vegetables out of the fridge to stir-fry and grabbed packets of instant noodles from the pantry.

O'Halloran joined her by the stove. "I'm no chef, but if you want stir-fried vegetables, I can do that."

She handed him a knife and board then put the noodles on to cook.

While O'Halloran chopped, Jenna got out the wok and some oil, and set it to heat. Carter and Mc-

Cabe found plates and cutlery and set the table, while O'Halloran cooked the vegetables. Minutes later, Jenna extracted the take-out containers from the oven that were filled with now sadly wilted Chinese and placed them on the table. Along with the large bowl of noodles and the stir-fried vegetables, there was enough food, but barely.

Her heart pounded just a little faster as O'Halloran held her chair for her then took the seat next to hers. He wasn't sitting any closer to her than Carter on her other side, but she couldn't help being ultra-sensitive to his presence.

From the moment he had stepped back inside the house after chasing the intruder, O'Halloran had been sticking close.

At first, she had thought it was just his natural protective streak. She had gotten hurt while in his care, so of course he would be careful that nothing further happened to her.

But his behaviour wasn't just about protection. From the time McCabe and his two friends had arrived, O'Halloran had made no bones about bluntly staking his claim on her in front of the other men. And since that kiss he had constantly invaded her personal space.

The physical closeness signalled a major step into uncharted territory with O'Halloran, and the message he was sending was loud and clear. She could delay the issue all she liked, but unless she came up with a definitive *no*, sex was going to enter the equation.

It was no longer a matter of *if* so much as *when*.

Marc ate slowly but steadily, despite his hunger, more aware of Jenna—the pure, elegant line of her profile, the faint flowery perfume that clung to her skin—than the taste of the food on his plate.

His phone vibrated. Excusing himself, he walked out into the hall and took the call. It was Farrell. They had checked out the registration plate and it belonged to a security company. They had rung the firm and one of the guys had just gone down to the compound and checked. The van wasn't in the compound. It had been left out on the road, with the keys under the mat.

Grimly, Marc hung up and walked back into the kitchen and related the news.

When McCabe heard the name of the firm he looked interested. "They do installations. I'll give Williams, the guy who runs it, a call. He'll let me look at his employee roster."

Carter picked up plates and carried them to the counter. "If the van was left outside of the compound, there's got to be some security footage."

Marc slipped his phone into his pocket. "Farrell's already covered that angle. Whoever used the van was smart enough to park away from the surveilled area."

West raised a brow. "So the guy returned the vehicle *and* knew where the cameras were. It's got to be one of the employees."

Jenna set her fork down and began stacking empty serving dishes. "Or someone in the security business, who's got access. If it helps, I've got a partial photo of him on my camera."

Marc suddenly thought of something that hadn't happened earlier in the evening, which should have. He caught Jenna's gaze. "When you left the house today, did you set your alarm?"

"It was on. I never leave the house, even to go for a walk, without setting it."

"When we got to the house the power was on, so the alarm was working."

She caught his drift immediately. "The alarm was set, but it didn't go off, even though he was inside the house when we got here."

Security alarms. He felt as if a piece of the puzzle had just fallen into place, crazily linking what was happening to Jenna even more strongly with his own investigation into Natalie's and Jared's deaths.

In that instant, he remembered why the guy wearing the ball cap at the cemetery the previous day had looked familiar. A couple of months earlier when he had been researching the firm that had installed the security alarm in his house, which had burned down, an employee in a ball cap had been spooked by his presence and had left in a hurry.

Marc had hit a brick wall when it had turned out that the guy he had seen wasn't an employee of the firm. He had assumed that whoever it was had probably been a customer who had recognized him as an ex-cop and made a quick exit. It happened occasionally, so he had written off that particular episode.

But not anymore.

The guy who was stalking Jenna wore a ball cap. It was a small point, but it was too much of a coincidence for him to ignore.

"That seals it. The odds are our boy works in security, probably selling or installing systems."

There was no other explanation. The man had bypassed Jenna's alarm, which was a good one, so that probably meant he knew his way around the interior wiring, or he had access to the manufacturer's master codes. First thing in the morning he would arrange to have the alarm removed and taken in for fingerprinting then have a new system installed.

Jenna walked through to her office, found her handbag and looked for her phone so she could provide the guys with copies of the photo. When she couldn't find the phone, she rummaged through the bag to double-check.

She became aware that O'Halloran was leaning against the doorjamb. "The phone's gone."

"Maybe you left it in your car."

"No. I always carry my phone in a side pocket in my handbag, specifically so I don't forget it."

A flash of memory came back to haunt her; the moment she had been spooked earlier, the creaking floorboards. "He was in here. I thought he must have been after my laptop, but it makes more sense that he was after the phone."

"And the photograph. Too bad we already downloaded a copy at Auckland Central. What kind of phone was it?"

Jenna set the bag down on her desk, suppressing the queasy desire to empty the contents of her bag on her desk and wipe everything down. Whoever he was, he had been wearing gloves, so his skin hadn't actually touched anything she owned; somehow that fact was important.

Jenna supplied the make of the phone. A quick rummage and she found the box and the book that went with it.

O'Halloran checked out the specs. "It's got Blue-tooth and a GPS. Is your wireless connection active?"

"I never turn it off. When I'm away from my desk, the phone's my portable office."

"Good. I'll give this to West. He's got shares in a phone network and some scary software he developed for the military. If he can get an access code, we should be able to remotely activate the GPS function on the phone."

A flurry of rain hit her office windows. The cold air that went with the building storm seemed to seep through the glass. Jenna rubbed at her arms, to stave off the chill.

Her jaw clenched when she noticed that her hands were doing the shaking thing again.

O'Halloran said something soft beneath his breath, laced his fingers through hers and pulled her into a loose clinch.

Surprise gave way to warmth and tingling heat, pushing back the reaction that had gripped her when she had realized *he* had taken the phone.

She let out a breath and tried to relax, dropping her forehead on O'Halloran's shoulder and breathing in his scent. O'Halloran's palm curved around her nape, the fiery heat comforting.

The phone was just a possession. It could be replaced easily enough. It was the underlining of the fact that the stalker had been in her home and had systematically gone through her things—the sense of violation—that had upset her.

After a few seconds, when O'Halloran seemed content to simply hold her, she finally began to relax.

O'Halloran responded by easing her close enough

that one thigh slid between his and her breasts flattened against his chest. She could feel the masculine shape of him against one hip, but the semi-arousal aside, the hug still felt more about comfort than sex.

The fierce tension that had gripped her left her by degrees, making her aware of just how tightly strung she had been. Letting out a breath, she relaxed a little more, enjoying the feeling of being cocooned by O'Halloran's heat and strength.

His hand squeezed gently at her nape, adding to the delicious feeling of comfort. "I know it's a shock," he murmured. "The bastard's invaded your home and he seems to want to mess with your head, but he's not that smart. He's made mistakes, and he'll make more, guaranteed."

She tipped back her head and met his gaze. "How long does the GPS have to be on to pinpoint the location?"

"If we're scanning for the phone, all it needs is enough time to make the connection with the server, and we'll have the location."

Despite the comfort O'Halloran had been dispensing, his expression was grim and cold enough to send a shiver down her spine, although this time in a good way.

The guy who had broken into her home had thought he was targeting a lone, vulnerable woman. But with O'Halloran now in the picture she was abruptly certain that her stalker had bitten off way more than he could chew.

Chapter 12

After McCabe, Carter and West had left, Jenna locked the door. O'Halloran was still in the house. He was making calls and had his laptop booted up on her kitchen table, so she wasn't alone. The act of locking up should have made her feel safe, but she was suddenly all too aware that she wasn't safe in her own home and that she couldn't stay there tonight.

The thought of trying to sleep in her bedroom filled her with quiet dread. She hadn't cleaned up all of the pottery shards and broken glass. In any case, it would take a while to wipe the attack from her mind.

Once O'Halloran had checked through her email and her folder of negative fan mail, she would pack what she needed and check in to a hotel somewhere.

The act of making a decision, of taking back control, was steadying. Feeling calmer, she walked up to her room and stepped inside, tensing at the mess and the blank, cold view out onto her balcony.

Flicking on a light, she marched across to the French doors, checked the locks and drew the curtains. As she turned, she caught her reflection in her dresser mirror and caught her breath.

She was used to seeing herself casually neat, her hair brushed or coiled and, for want of a better word, *calm*.

In the space of a couple of hours, that had all changed.

Her hair was tousled, her face pale, but it was her mouth that drew her attention. Her lips were pale but a little swollen. She looked like she had just been kissed. Or as if she had just rolled out of bed.

Grabbing a loose jacket, she shrugged into it then dragged a brush through her hair and pinned it up into a coil. Unfortunately, with her new cut, the shorter tendrils wouldn't stick and cascaded around her jaw and nape, the effect somehow even sexier than just leaving her hair loose.

Sex. The thought—the hot, sweaty skin-on-skin reality of it—sent a quiver of sensation through her.

Putting the brush down, she stared at her reflection. The problem was, she thought grimly, that for O'Halloran casual sex might be no big deal, but for her it would be.

She was used to being solitary and alone. She worked alone, ate alone, slept alone.

A graphic image of what it would be like to go to bed with O'Halloran, to be naked with him on top, flashed through her on a wave of heat.

She realized how enclosed and "female" her world had become. She worked, exercised and socialised with women. Even her accountant and doctor were both female. The only contact she had with men was, literally, by chance, through her fan mail or the occasional date she got talked into. And none of those men were even remotely in O'Halloran's league.

Retrieving her laptop from beneath her mattress, she walked back downstairs. She collected the file from the bottom drawer of her desk and carried it all through to the lounge.

A Victorian carriage clock sitting on her mantel informed her that it wasn't late, barely ten o'clock, which was disorienting. After everything that had happened, it felt closer to midnight.

In the kitchen, she could hear the deep, cool sound of O'Halloran's voice as he talked on the phone. He would be leaving soon, but before he left, she wanted to show him the emails.

As she was booting up the computer, she remembered the conversation with Selene, and her conviction that her favourite fan could provide a clue to the identity of the stalker.

Offhand, she didn't think Lydell88 was stalker material. The conviction was knee-jerk, because every online or email conversation she'd had with Lydell had been positive and uplifting: she liked him. If he was a stalker, she was certain those traits would have revealed themselves over the years of correspondence, and they hadn't.

The other reason she didn't think it could be him was that he never pushed contact. Usually he only instigated a conversation when she had a book out. She in turn tried to limit her contacts to the times she needed police procedural information.

Placing the laptop on the coffee table, she booted it up and considered lighting the fire. It wasn't that cold, but with rain drumming on the windows and the wind building in intensity, the flickering flames would add a comforting glow.

Satisfied that the laptop battery was good for a couple of hours, she found her fan mail file, selected the one labelled Lydell and opened it up.

A few minutes later, O'Halloran joined her.

He flicked through a couple of the emails but didn't seem overly interested in Lydell, other than the fact that she had kept every email Lydell88 had ever sent.

Marc closed down Jenna's Lydell email file and opened her folder of negative fan mail and stared at the print copy of the email that contained her threat. He experienced the same cold sense of a missing piece of a puzzle dropping into place that he'd felt the first time he read the email.

Memory flickered, a series of freeze frames that made him go still inside.

Natalie sitting at her computer most nights when he had gotten in late. The argument when he had discovered that she was chatting with an online friend. A male friend.

Jenna frowned. "What is it?"

"I've seen that email address before, or something very like it. There's one change, an extra letter tagged on the end."

Maybe it was sheer chance, coincidence, and this was a completely different person, but he didn't think so. When he'd worked cases at Auckland Central and made a breakthrough he had felt the same sharp kick of instinct, the same inner certainty.

His decision at the cemetery to refocus his own personal investigation on Natalie's and Jenna's lives was confirmed. For six years, he had centered his hunt for the person who had killed his family on a criminal ring he had been investigating at the time. His spectacular lack of success was now explained. He had assumed that his house being torched was a crime of vengeance, directed at him.

Normally he worked only on facts. But in the aftermath of funerals and the slow, painful recovery from his injuries, he had made the fundamental mistake of making an assumption.

Now, finally, that assumption, which had stonewalled his investigation, had been cleared away. Marc hadn't been the target of the perpetrator. The murderer's focus had been Natalie.

"You've found something."

The flat certainty in Jenna's voice brought Marc's head up. He controlled his impatient need to start work on a list of men in both Jenna's and Natalie's pasts. If Hansen managed to match the fingerprints, that would be a step that was no longer required.

"That the criminals I thought were responsible for Natalie's and Jared's deaths, weren't."

The room seemed to fill with silence, punctuated by the slow tick of an antique clock.

"I'll make coffee."

Too tense to sit, Marc levered himself up from the couch and restlessly paced the length of the sitting room, his mind switching to the avalanche of new information that had, within the space of a few hours, changed everything.

He found himself staring at a small trio of family snapshots on an elegant corner table—one of the silver frames held a studio photograph of Natalie with their small son.

His chest tightened. He hadn't murdered them, but for years guilt had eaten at him. He had assumed they had died because of his work as a police detective.

The need to absolve himself, if only partially, had driven him to continue to search for evidence. He had hunted a phantom, one who had constantly slipped from his grasp.

The perp had been content to taunt Marc from a distance. But, finally, he had made a mistake. Probably because Jenna was a woman and lived alone, he had fallen into the trap of underestimating her.

The fact that he had turned up in person was a major breakthrough.

Marc now had motivation, an email, a photograph, video footage and, most importantly, with the cellophane on the rose, and the clipboard and pen he had found at the base of Jenna's fence, fingerprints.

Despite all of the fancy evidence-collection techniques that were so popular on TV shows, fingerprints remained the number-one method of obtaining a conviction. There was just no way of getting around the fact that fingerprints placed the perp at the scene of the crime.

Although none of the evidence was conclusive unless they got a match on the prints, and that might not happen. But at least he finally had enough information to put together a profile and prove that a murder had occurred.

Marc's jaw tightened. For the first time, he could see the man he'd been searching for.

By running a list of the men both Natalie and Jenna knew, by virtue of cross matching, he could isolate a list of suspects.

Then there was the aspect of Jenna's book. Something Jenna had included in her latest story had pushed a button, strongly enough that the perp had tried to intimidate her into removing the book from the market.

A sense of icy satisfaction filled Marc. He would go back through the book with a fine-tooth comb. Somewhere, there was information vital enough that the perp had seen the possibility of exposure and had moved to nullify the risk.

Jenna strolled back into the room and set a tray down on the coffee table. Marc set the photograph down and walked toward Jenna. As he did so, he became sharply aware that in the space of the few minutes it had taken her to make coffee, something had changed.

The glow of awareness was gone from her expression, turned off as efficiently as turning off a tap.

Jenna handed him one of the mugs, but instead of sitting next to him on the sofa, she retreated to an armchair, further emphasising the distance between them.

Frowning, Marc drank a mouthful of the coffee. "Natalie used to chat to some guy online. I'm pretty sure it's the same guy who emailed you."

Grimly, he noted that Jenna didn't look as surprised as she should have. "You knew she was talking to someone. That Natalie was involved with some guy online."

Shock jerked Jenna's head up. "I didn't know about the online part. All I knew was that she had met someone. She didn't say how."

"If Natalie was involved with someone then you need to tell me all the details. Forget that she and I were married."

The calm flatness of O'Halloran's tone was faintly chilling. ·

Keeping Nat's little secret had been a habit, made easy by her death. The way Jenna had seen it, you shouldn't have to tell on people after they had died, but she couldn't afford to hold back now. If Nat's illicit boyfriend and Jenna's stalker were one and the same, then that was a bona fide link.

"Natalie phoned me the day before she died to tell me she was considering leaving you to be with her new boyfriend. I didn't quite believe her." She shook her head. "I couldn't believe she would—"

O'Halloran picked up the copy of the email. "I need to know his name."

The remoteness of his gaze made the breath catch in the back of her throat. "She never gave me a name, but I didn't know he was an *online* friend. All I knew was that he had been sending her gifts and that Nat was… excited. She died the next day."

Jenna's stomach tightened. She literally felt sick at the implications. Now that it seemed clear that the house fire hadn't been set by the serial arsonist, the meeting with Natalie's online friend had taken on a new, potentially ominous cast. That didn't mean he was implicated in the murder, but he could be.

It was a connection she should have made and hadn't. The dangers of meeting someone off the internet swirled around in her head. She knew better than most how many crazies there were out there.

"Don't beat yourself up about it. I knew about the online friend, and I didn't connect him."

The flat acceptance in his voice stopped her in her tracks. She knew that Natalie hadn't been entirely happy in the marriage, but she had assumed that was because she had suffered from postnatal depression after having the baby.

She had never considered that O'Halloran might not have been happy. "I don't know. Maybe it was just talk. In any event there was no point mentioning it, because nothing happened—she didn't go with him."

And Jenna hadn't wanted to destroy his memories of Nat. After all, she hadn't done anything wrong. After she had died, the last thing she had wanted to do was despoil her cousin's memory.

O'Halloran was silent for a beat. "There was if he had anything to do with the gas explosion."

A chill went through Jenna at the soft, flat comment. On the heels of that another thought made her go still inside. "I used a couple of the things that happened to Natalie in *Deadly Valentine*, the secret admirer and the use of arson. If he's the same man, that would explain why he's so angry."

Because she had inadvertently revealed his crime, even if only in a fictionalised form.

Pushing to his feet, O'Halloran slid his phone out of his pocket. "Which will be why he wants your phone and computer, and anything else that might connect him to Natalie's death."

He short-dialled Farrell. When he got her voice mail, he left a message and hung up.

A heavy roll of thunder indicated that the storm had moved overhead. As Jenna pulled a curtain aside to stare outside, Marc gave in to impulse and walked over to her. He shouldn't touch her, but he found himself wanting to pull her close and soothe away the tension that was visible in the line of her back, the set of her jaw.

Her inability to meet his gaze brought his head up, sharpened all of his senses. In that moment, the small body language cues he had noted ever since the encounter at the gravesite—her pale face and abrupt change of mood when he had focused on Natalie—added up to a conclusion he should have arrived at earlier. Somehow, despite the passage of years and the fact that she had been the one who had ended it, Jenna still cared for him.

Cancel that: nine years had passed. She loved him.

Her shuttered gaze met his. Something about his expression must have alerted her that he knew, because she smiled brightly. "I'll make a copy of a couple of Lydell88's emails, if you want them."

"Great idea." Maybe it would stop him from doing something rash like reaching out, snagging her wrist and pulling her close again.

Jaw tight, he watched Jenna collect the file and walk out of the room.

The thought that they were close to lovemaking momentarily wiped his mind clean of anything else. The fierceness of his response set him on guard.

With the investigation now heating up, staying close to Jenna, and allowing her memory, and his, to unlock, could be the most effective way to finally capture the murderer who had eluded him for six years.

Like it or not, Jenna had become the key to solving the case. He couldn't afford to be separate from her right now.

If he made love with Jenna, maintaining any kind of professional distance would be impossible and, with the stalker now a tangible threat, he needed to maintain his clarity of mind.

Satisfaction eased off some of his tension. Decision made.

He wanted Jenna in his bed. And she wanted him, but they would have to wait. Protecting Jenna and making progress on the investigation had to take precedence.

He had already lost Natalie and Jared.

He couldn't lose Jenna.

Chapter 13

Jenna stepped back into the room just as the lights went out.

"Wait here," O'Halloran said quietly. "I'm going to check the fuse box, just in case."

She heard the faint sound of his footfall, felt the displacement of air as he glided past.

Not wanting to sit alone in the dark with the sound of thunder rolling overhead, she followed O'Halloran out into the hall and watched as he shone his flashlight into the fuse box. "It looks okay."

She trailed him to the kitchen and watched as he shrugged into the shoulder holster. The metallic click as he slid the clip home in the Glock sent a chill down her spine. She had watched O'Halloran unload the gun and place both the gun and shoulder holster on the kitchen counter; she just hadn't thought he would have to use it.

He paused at the kitchen door. "I won't be long. The whole street is in darkness, so he hasn't tampered with the power this time. I think this outage is genuine. A bolt of lightning probably knocked out the transformer."

The kitchen door shut behind him. Her spine tingled at the silent way O'Halloran had moved through the darkness. Unnerved by being alone in the dark, she found the penlight she had used earlier.

Swinging the beam around the kitchen, just to make sure she *was* still alone, she walked quickly to the kitchen door, opened it and stepped out onto the back porch. A blast of cold air and rain instantly soaked her.

O'Halloran ghosted in out of the pitch-blackness, his eyes shooting dark fire. "What are you doing outside?"

Jaw taut, Jenna ignored the question. She was in no mood to explain that after the episode with the stalker in the so-called safety of her house, outside had seemed a whole lot safer. "Did you find anything?"

"He's not on the property." O'Halloran stepped beneath the porch and slicked wet hair back from his face. His shirt was plastered to his shoulders, water trickled down his chin.

Lightning lit up the back garden with a searing white glow, and, a split second later, a crack of thunder made her jump.

He stepped inside, found the towel that he had used earlier and blotted his face and hair. "That's it," he said grimly. "You can't stay here. We can't stay in my apartment, either, because I can't guarantee that he doesn't know where I live, which means a hotel."

Jenna stepped into O'Halloran's apartment, a brief stop-off on the way to a hotel, while he packed a bag.

Curiously, she looked around as he led the way through a large modern apartment with vaulted ceilings and dark hardwood floors softened by rich Turkish rugs. Warm lamplight glowed, pooling softly over comfortable sofas and highlighting an array of interesting oils on the walls.

They stepped into a wide hallway. The white walls, which would have been uncomfortably sterile if left bare, again, were adorned with an interesting collection of paintings. "I didn't know you liked art."

He paused by the doorway to a bedroom. "I like it. I just don't know anything about it. Luckily, my mother solves that problem. Every year she runs a charity art auction. I donate, and she insists on turning the donation into a bid on a painting."

Jenna stared at the delicate watercolours lining the hall. They all matched and she was suddenly certain that O'Halloran was well aware of that fact.

The paintings gave Jenna an odd, narrow glance into O'Halloran's family life. She knew from the careful selection that his mother had done her best to decorate his walls with light and beauty, and to turn the sterile barn O'Halloran had chosen, the very antithesis of a family home, into a comfortable apartment. And O'Halloran had let her.

The fact that O'Halloran's mother had a hand in decorating also told her that O'Halloran lived alone.

The thought was oddly disturbing. She was used to living alone. As a writer, solitude suited her for the most part, but O'Halloran was different. Despite his occupation as a cop, she had always considered him to be a family man.

It was an odd moment to take her head out of the

sand and confront her phobia about being involved with either a soldier or a cop, because it was a fact that they needed their families more than most. The thought that at the end of a day of dealing with hardened criminals and maybe even the rawness of death, O'Halloran had come home to a cold, empty apartment made her chest squeeze tight.

Despite the art on the walls, the apartment was hollow, and it was lonely.

Within minutes, O'Halloran had what he needed. Glad to be leaving the too-revealing confines of his apartment, Jenna climbed back into his vehicle.

She studied street signs as he accelerated out of the center of town and found an on-ramp to the Southern motorway. "So…where are we going?"

He checked the rearview mirror then flipped open the glove compartment and extracted an accommodation booklet, which he handed to her. "Find a hotel or motel. I'm just going to drive for a while and make sure we're not being followed."

Half an hour later, feeling exhausted, Jenna walked into the double-room suite she had booked in the Lombard Hotel.

O'Halloran stepped in beside her and put their bags down. "Choose the room you want and I'll take the other."

Minutes later, after placing her bag in the nearest room and making a brief survey of the suite, which had a small kitchen, Jenna took a shower, changed for bed and brushed her teeth.

While she was in the bathroom, she took stock of her bruises. The ones around her neck hadn't developed much beyond red marks, so hopefully they would fade by morning, but her knee was a different matter. The dark bruise was large and spectacular, and the knee was still sore.

After rubbing in some arnica, which she'd brought with her, she quickly dried her hair then walked through the lounge to her bedroom. On the way, she glimpsed a slice of tanned torso as O'Halloran peeled out of his shirt. At that moment, his gaze snagged on hers for long enough that she froze in place and her stomach clenched. Then he looked away.

Cheeks burning, feeling like a love-starved voyeur, Jenna continued on toward her bedroom, closed her door and slid into bed. Flicking off the light, she lay in darkness and tried to relax, but her heart was still racing. She hadn't mistaken O'Halloran's initial response. His gaze had been narrowed and she had gotten the impression that he hadn't minded in the least that she was seeing him with his shirt off.

Somewhere in the distance she could hear O'Halloran taking a shower. Every time she thought about the comprehensive way O'Halloran had kissed her back at her house she melted down, although he hadn't pushed any further. Sometime during the evening he had seemed to back off, leaving her floating in limbo.

It didn't take a rocket scientist to figure out when and why the change had happened. When O'Halloran had made the connection about Natalie's online friend, his whole focus had altered.

She had felt his instant shift away from her and back to Natalie and Jared. When she'd seen him staring at Nat's photo, she had gotten the message loud and clear. No matter how focused O'Halloran was on investigating her stalking and protecting her—no matter how seductive that seemed—she couldn't allow herself to forget that his primary motivation was the same one that had driven him for the past six years. The need to solve the murder of his wife and child.

As powerful and overwhelming as the attraction was for her, she couldn't allow herself to forget that to O'Halloran her primary importance was as a lead in his investigation.

The following evening, after a day split between Auckland Central and putting together a comprehensive list of all of the men in both Natalie's and Jenna's lives, Marc surveyed the reception room at the Lombard Hotel. A combined book signing and literacy function was being held and the room was presently packed with an array of brightly dressed and heavily perfumed women. Because the hotel was also a casino, a smattering of other guests continually drifted through the door and mingled, a number of them men.

West and Carter were present, cruising the crowd and keeping an eye on the doors. Blade Lombard, part of the SAS team that Carter, West and McCabe had belonged to, and also the current manager of the hotel and casino, had also offered to help out with security.

Like Marc, Blade's gaze was fixed on the line of fans queuing to obtain a signed book from Jenna. A number of other authors were also part of the function, but none of them commanded queues that wound like a snake around the walls.

He caught Marc's eye, his own expression rueful. "Do you read her books?"

Marc automatically stiffened then allowed himself to relax. "Yeah, they're good."

"My wife writes the same stuff. I like her books, although the love scenes are a bit—"

Marc found himself grinning that Blade, who was normally eloquent, seemed to be at a loss for words.

Blade frowned as he saw what Marc had just noticed: a very masculine-looking woman wearing a heavy dress and a shapeless jacket was in Jenna's queue. "Do you think she's for real?"

Marc's jaw tightened as he noted her brawny shoulders and muscular calves. "What do you think?"

Blade shook his head. "No way."

By tacit agreement they moved closer, Blade strolling down one side of the queue, Marc taking the other. Marc still wasn't completely sure of gender, but he wasn't about to be caught flatfooted.

As the woman reached Jenna's table, her hand dived inside the left lapel of her jacket. Marc swore beneath his breath. A split second later, Blade, who was slightly closer and definitely more on edge, beat him to the punch and caught the woman in a wrestling hold. A strangled shriek rent the air as Marc jerked the flap of the jacket open and the "gun," in reality a battered copy of what looked like Jenna's first book, dropped to the floor. Jenna, looking gorgeous and sultry in a tangerine halter-neck dress, pushed to her feet.

The whole room seemed to freeze as the motorised click of cameras filled the air. Blade muttered a gritty, mostly indistinct word and let her go, and the now overloud hum of conversation broke over them.

The woman spun and confronted her attacker. "You're Blade Lombard, aren't you?"

Blade dragged at his tie, looking acutely uncomfortable. "That's right, ma'am."

"I read your wife's books."

A relieved expression flashed in his dark gaze. "How many copies would you like?"

The woman smiled determinedly. "I don't want a book. What I'd like is for you to do that hold again so I can get a picture."

"How about," Jenna interceded smoothly, "I give you a gift pack of all ten of my books?" She grabbed a wrapped box of books and handed it over. The woman, now thoroughly distracted, took the books. Blade, recognizing an out when he saw one, slipped away into the crowd.

With the woman mollified by the books, Jenna indicated to Marc that she needed to take a break. On edge, even though there hadn't been a threat, Marc stayed close as he walked Jenna to the ladies' room.

Jenna sent him a cool glance. "Did you have to attack her?"

"I'm not taking any chances."

Jenna was abruptly silent, and Marc cursed himself for being so grim. Up until now, Jenna had actually relaxed and she had been enjoying herself.

The corridor leading to the bathrooms was filled with a mixture of men. On top of the casino crowd, there was also a pharmacy convention running in an adjacent reception room.

Gaze cold as he skimmed each of the men, Marc made an executive decision. He couldn't afford to let Jenna go into the ladies' room without protection. Ignoring outraged gasps, he stepped into the pale pink bathroom and grimly waited.

As they exited the ladies' room, a barrage of cameras

met them. His annoyance growing, a cold itch down his spine, Marc escorted Jenna back to her table. Using his lip mike, he spoke to West and Carter and requested that they move in closer and watch anyone with a camera. A few years ago, McCabe had been shot at a fashion event filled with cameras. Just like the book signing, the fashion show had been a security nightmare.

Jenna's queue gradually reduced in size. Marc checked his watch as he grimly stood over Jenna, more than happy to make it plain that if anyone tried to harm her they would have to deal with him. The fact that more and more men had filtered into the room didn't make him feel any happier.

A pretty female reporter for a women's magazine asked if she could take a picture of Jenna. After Jenna had posed, she requested a second shot, this time with Marc.

Obligingly, Jenna looped one arm around his waist. Cameras whirred and clicked as more reporters moved in. In that moment, something shifted at the edge of Marc's vision, a reporter with a zoom lens that looked more like a gun than a camera, and his patience dissolved.

Chapter 14

Expression grim, O'Halloran's hand landed in the small of her back. "That's it, we're out of here."

West and Carter automatically fell in behind them. Somewhere, another camera flashed.

O'Halloran's jaw locked. He saw the distinctive outline of Blade Lombard's shoulders, the black gleam of his ponytail, heard a muffled epithet. A number of reporters had been asked to leave. At a guess, another had just been escorted to the door.

They reached the bank of elevators, and O'Halloran pressed the call button. Slow seconds passed before the doors swished open and he ushered Jenna inside. Carter stepped inside with them; West stayed downstairs. O'Halloran lifted a hand as the doors closed. West would keep an eye on anyone trying to follow them.

O'Halloran's arm locked around Jenna's waist as the

elevator shot up. Jenna didn't complain. She'd been on tenterhooks all night, mostly because of the danger, but also because O'Halloran had been the cynosure of a lot of female eyes and she'd finally had enough.

She had thought she could be adult and sophisticated about O'Halloran mixing with her mostly female audience, but a gorgeous, leggy brunette coiling her arms around O'Halloran's neck had been the last straw.

Natalie had been the exception to the rule, because she had been genuinely nice and Jenna had loved her, but with any other woman she found she was burningly, searingly jealous.

O'Halloran hadn't responded to the brunette—he had barely seemed to see her—but that didn't matter. The fact was, she had been a threat. For however long she and O'Halloran were together, he was *her* man, and she wasn't prepared to share.

Carter melted away as they reached their suite. O'Halloran unlocked the door then insisted on going in first.

O'Halloran's actions were like a dash of cold water, forcibly reminding Jenna of the threat. Following him into the suite, she closed the door behind her and leaned against it as she waited for O'Halloran to finish checking it out.

He stepped out of her bedroom, crossed the width of the lounge and looked in the second bedroom.

When he re-joined her in the lounge, he shrugged out of the shoulder holster and laid it and the Glock on the coffee table beside his laptop. Dragging his tie to loosen it, he simply walked to her and pulled her into his arms. Dropping her evening bag on the floor, Jenna closed her arms around his neck, went up on her toes and angled her jaw for his kiss.

After the past twenty or so hours, when O'Halloran had seemed to withdraw from her almost completely into the investigation and his role as bodyguard, she had begun to despair. She had understood his motivation, his driving need to bring the killer to justice, but she hadn't liked the feeling of being so easily sidelined.

They were going to make love, and the knowledge that they had finally reached that point made her feel wobbly with relief. After the misery of the previous night, spent tossing and turning in her room, considering the very real possibility that once the killer was caught O'Halloran could walk out of her life, there was no way she was missing a chance that might never come again.

From the time she had fished her latest book out of its box and been shocked by the likeness of the cover model to O'Halloran until now, her objections to falling for him had been systematically obliterated. Maybe it was as simple as recognizing just how lonely *she* had been. Whatever the catalyst was, inside she had changed and she couldn't change back.

She wanted him; she loved him, and the emotions were deep and painful.

She could back away from committing to sex, insist they wait and see if a viable relationship developed. The only problem was, neither of them was "normal" when it came to relationships.

They were both hurt and just a little dysfunctional. She had loved him for years. If she had loved him that long, chances were she wasn't going to fall out of love with him anytime soon.

Maybe what they would share wouldn't mean anything special to O'Halloran. The probability was that for him it would be nothing more than a fleeting affair.

Even so, that was a risk she had to take. She couldn't live with herself if she didn't at least try.

O'Halloran lifted his head, his gaze midnight dark. "If you don't want this, tell me now."

For an answer, Jenna fitted herself more tightly against the hard-muscled plains of O'Halloran's body, and pulled his mouth back to hers.

The passion was white-hot and instant. The relief of her breasts flattened against his chest, the scrape of stubble against her jaw, made her shudder. O'Halloran tasted as good as he smelled, clean and male and delicious.

As she lifted up against him for a second kiss, this one deeper, hotter, she wondered how she had managed to live without him.

His fingers tangled in her hair, holding her captive. She logged his groan of satisfaction as his mouth came back down on hers, and she found herself walked back a half step, then another, until her bare back came up against the cold solidity of the wall.

The relief of O'Halloran's weight pinning her, the heat blasting off him, the firm shape of his arousal pressing into her belly, sent a sensation jerking through her. She felt his fingers at her nape, the release of tension as the halter of her dress loosened then slipped down to hang around her waist, then his hands swept up to cup her breasts.

For a brief moment, time seemed to move with liquid slowness as he kissed her jaw, the curve of her neck.

The abrasive warmth of his palms, the sensual drag of his shirt against naked skin, made her stomach clench.

Dragging at his tie, she tossed it aside and unfastened his shirt.

O'Halloran said something low and rough. Bending his head he took one breast in his mouth. Her fingers clenched in his hair for long seconds then restlessly shifted to his shoulders as the aching heat in her belly coiled tight, and suddenly there was no air.

Jenna felt a tug, a rush of cool air, then fabric puddled around her feet.

Swallowing at the sheer vulnerability of being mostly naked while O'Halloran was still almost fully dressed, Jenna tugged at the buttons of his shirt until it hung loose from his shoulders. "I could do with some help here."

O'Halloran grinned quick and hard and shrugged out of the shirt then pulled her close. The heat of skin-on-skin contact spun her back nine years, to darkness and moonlight, an uncomfortable couch and too little time.

This time, she thought a little dizzily, as she dragged at the fastening of his trousers, they would have all night. She heard his swiftly indrawn breath, and then the room tilted as he swung her into his arms. Short seconds later, she found herself deposited on the cloud-like softness of the bed.

The room was dark, illuminated by the strip of light glowing in the door and by the bright moonlight flowing in off the balcony. She watched as O'Halloran stepped out of his trousers. She drew in her breath at the sleek width of his shoulders, the hard flatness of his stomach, the muscular length of his legs.

She heard a faint tearing sound. Dimly, she regis-

tered that O'Halloran had just sheathed himself with
a condom.

She felt a tug at her hips and registered the glide
of her panties as they slid down her legs and the cool
wash of air.

For long minutes he simply held her close, kissing
and soothing her and letting her explore. When her
hand slid down over washboard abs and found him, he
groaned and came down on top of her. She wrapped
her arms around his neck, pulling him close. He lowered his weight, and her breath came in as she felt the
nudge of his knee between her thighs.

Her stomach tightened at the sheer vulnerability of
opening her legs, but that consideration evaporated as
she felt the sudden pressure as he lodged in her opening. His gaze locked with hers as his weight settled
more heavily on her.

The sheer intimacy of being this close with O'Halloran,
gazes locked, breaths mingling, the sensual heat of his
body pressing into hers, was seductive. She arched, wanting more, wanting him closer still, and with one heavy
thrust he was inside her.

Time seemed to slow, stop, as she adjusted to the
intrusion, part of her still reeling from the unexpected
speed of his entry.

O'Halloran cupped her jaw, his gaze strained. "When
was the last time you made love?"

Jenna sucked in a breath, her whole being still cen-
tred on easing the pressure between her legs. "Do I
have to answer that?"

O'Halloran said something low and gritty. "I knew
it. You haven't made love with anyone else."

She took another breath and moved her hips slightly. The pressure was easing, but just. "I've been…busy."

"Uh-huh. Writing about it."

She caught the edge of his smile, and the tension that had gripped her at the whole idea of making love evaporated. After all, it wasn't an exam she could potentially fail; it was something that was supposed to come naturally.

He cupped her jaw. "If you want me to stop, just say so. Otherwise, I'll take it slow."

Her gaze flashed to his. "Don't you dare stop."

In response, O'Halloran leaned down and touched his mouth to hers, the kiss oddly sweet. As he did so, he eased back then pushed in slowly. This time the entry was easier, smoother. O'Halloran continued the slow rocking for long minutes. Dipping his head, he took one breast into his mouth and bit down gently.

Sensation gathered, coiled tight, jerked through her in hot, dizzying waves. She gripped O'Halloran's shoulders. Moments later, he plunged deep and the room dissolved.

She must have fallen asleep, because when she woke, O'Halloran was withdrawing himself from her body by slow increments. He eased his weight off her fully and left the bed. Shivering a little at the loss of his body heat and the cool air-conditioning flowing over her damp skin, she dragged the coverlet over her.

She heard O'Halloran's voice as he spoke to someone on his cell. Minutes later, he returned and slid into bed with her.

"That was Farrell. They couldn't match the prints with anyone from the security company."

Even though she was sleepy, her brain automatically clicked into investigative gear. "What about associate firms? Suppliers?"

"Farrell's got a list. That's what I was doing last night. The checking is going to take some legwork."

She yawned and blinked as an idea popped into her head. "What about the list of registration plate names? There were a couple of companies listed."

O'Halloran shook his head. "You should have been a cop. One of the companies is a security wholesaler. Farrell's getting a warrant and putting together a team. That should be a go in an hour or so."

Now wide-awake, Jenna watched as O'Halloran pulled on dark pants and, not bothering with a shirt, walked back out to the lounge. She listened to his deep, cool voice as he made another series of calls.

After a while, tiredness caught up with her and she drifted into a light doze. The next time she woke, O'Halloran was sliding back into bed. Pleasure hummed through her at the sheer, comfortable intimacy of having him in bed with her. It was something she could get used to. "Did you make progress?"

"Some."

The neutral tone to his voice, the subtle distance, informed her that the breakthrough was significant.

As hard as she tried to keep it at bay, a tension she didn't want to feel crept up on her, dissolving the warm bubble of happiness she had been inhabiting ever since they'd made love.

She should be happy for them both. Her stalker would be put behind bars, and O'Halloran would find Natalie and Jared's killer. They would both have closure.

While she knew that O'Halloran's distance was just a

part of him she had to accept, a knee-jerk reaction after years of keeping details of investigations confidential, she couldn't help but resent the barrier it represented. Just when she had managed to get a tiny piece of his attention, the investigation was taking him from her, but she wasn't about to give up without a fight.

Rolling on her side, she ran a hand over his torso and chest. Lifting up on her elbows, her hair falling in a curtain around her face, she dipped her head into the muscular curve of his neck, and breathed in his scent, then explored lower.

One big hand curled around her nape. "You don't want to sleep?"

"No."

"Good, I don't want to sleep, either."

Extracting another condom from the bedside table, he sheathed himself.

Her reaction was at odds with common sense. Condoms were good, any person with common sense wouldn't go near sex without one, unless they were married.

What she was feeling was silly, bordering on stupid, but a part of her hated it that O'Halloran had sheathed himself, because the condom seemed to symbolise his control.

The second the thought occurred to her, she wished it hadn't. For most of the evening, she'd been able to calmly ignore the fact that O'Halloran would probably never feel about her the way she did about him. But that didn't mean she had to put up with him deliberately controlling his passion, which she was suddenly sure was the case.

Gaze oddly wary, as if he had caught her mood, he

pulled her down until she was sprawled across his chest, and kissed her slowly and languorously.

She shifted, eased up his body and straddled him, taking control of the lovemaking and taking her time, absorbed by the sensations.

O'Halloran groaned. His hands framed her hips, adjusting the angle. She felt him lodge deeper and drew in a breath as he began to move. The idea of control crashed and burned as he rolled, pulling her beneath him, and once again the moonlit room spiralled away.

Branden Tell turned down his street and braked behind a dark sedan that seemed to be going nowhere fast. Either that or they were lost.

After trailing behind the car for long seconds, he put the lights of his Hummer on full beam, just to be obnoxious, and studied the two heads he had spotlighted.

Not kids looking for a place to park; they were both adults, one male, one female, and *she* was driving.

The woman checked him out in the rearview mirror, although with several hundred watts of high-powered halogen light hitting her square in the eyes, she wouldn't be able to make out a thing.

On the verge of forging past, she foiled him by speeding up. Tell swore beneath his breath and drove up hard behind them. They had a powerful car, but his Hummer would drive right over the top of them if he put his foot down.

They slowed, forcing him to brake again, although this time Tell controlled his temper, barely. His drive was just meters away—no point in losing it now—and besides, another car had nosed in behind him. If he wasn't mistaken it was a police cruiser.

An indicator light flashing jerked his attention back to the car in front. All the hairs at his nape lifted as the dark sedan turned into his drive.

Adrenaline shoving through him, he dipped his lights and drove past. His gaze glued to his rearview mirror, he watched the police cruiser park behind what he now knew was an unmarked police car.

He had been found.

Cold shock hit him.

His planning had been close to perfect. There was no way O'Halloran could connect him. He had never used an email address that could be traced to him, and fingerprint evidence was worthless since he had never been booked so his prints were not in the police system. If he needed a vehicle, he usually stole one, and the photo Whitmore had taken of him had also been worthless, because his hand had obscured most of his face.

The answer was clear. The bitch Whitmore must have found something on her computer.

A horn blared. His foot jerked down on the brake. The Hummer rocked to a halt, and he stared, disoriented, at the motorway intersection he had almost driven through.

Directing a one-finger salute at the car he had almost T-boned, he reversed, spun the wheel and headed back to town.

A pulse jumping at the side of his jaw, he drove into the Lombard Hotel car park and cruised around until he found O'Halloran's vehicle, which he had followed earlier in the day.

Satisfaction eased the cold fury that gripped him.

Somehow O'Halloran and Whitmore had found him

and sicced the cops on him. If he had arrived home a minute earlier, he would have been caught.

Although it didn't matter now. He was almost ready to leave.

Now he would finally get to be James Holden, the name on his fake passport. Once he was in his new life, Jenna Whitmore's book, O'Halloran and the murder investigation would no longer be a threat to him.

All he had to do was focus on the next few hours, carry through with his plan to pay back both Whitmore and O'Halloran, torch his warehouse and make it look like that loopy serial arsonist did it. It had worked for him once before, it would work again. Then he would leave on the first available flight out.

He drove until he found a parking space that afforded him a view of O'Halloran's vehicle and the exit lane.

It was the middle of the night, but if he didn't miss his guess, O'Halloran would be getting a call from the cops who were staking out his house. O'Halloran wouldn't be able to resist wanting a piece of the action. And if he had found his house, Tell was willing to bet the clever bastard had found his other bolt-hole.

A shame O'Halloran didn't know about the third one.

Dousing the Hummer's lights, Tell set himself to watch.

Chapter 15

The vibration of his phone brought O'Halloran out of a light doze.

Jenna moved sleepily as he slid his arm out from beneath her head, but she didn't wake. He padded out to the lounge, picked up his phone and texted West, who he'd arranged to meet down in the lobby.

Earlier in the evening, they'd managed to cross match the wholesaling company on the list of car registrations he had compiled with another firm that imported security alarms and the name that had come up had made all the hairs at the back of his neck stand on end.

Branden Tell was a name from his, Natalie's and Jenna's pasts. A sports jock with a number of minor disabilities, including colour-blindness and mild dyslexia, which had kept him out of the military and the police force, he had tried to date Natalie when she had been a student.

Marc hadn't thought of Tell because Natalie had been popular. The list of men who had wanted to date her had stretched from here to next week. He could remember Natalie commenting that she hadn't been interested in Tell, not because of the disabilities, but because he had been something of a cold fish until he had gotten her alone.

Finding Tell didn't make the past any easier to accept, but it had finally supplied Marc with a logical motivation for Natalie's and Jared's deaths.

Rejected by the military and the police, ultimately rejected by the woman he had wanted, Tell had decided to take revenge.

But Natalie hadn't been the only one Tell had targeted. Nine years ago he had taken Jenna out, on the night of the ball and she, too, had dumped him.

If he hadn't gotten worried and gone after Jenna with the intention of giving her a lift home, she would have been hit and killed or knocked into the river and drowned. Marc was willing to bet that the driver had been Tell and that, like the incident at the mall, he had meant to hit Jenna, both times.

He had called Farrell to bring her up-to-date with the development. She'd sent out a car, but evidently Tell hadn't been at his house or his place of work.

Not bothering to switch on a light, because his eyes were adjusted to the darkness and he didn't want to wake Jenna, he dressed quickly in a black T-shirt, pants and boots.

He shrugged into the dark webbing of his shoulder

harness, holstered the Glock, put on a loose black jacket and he was ready to go.

He walked to the bedroom door and checked on Jenna. Her hair was fanned out on the pillow, one arm draped over the end of the bed. His chest tightened as he noted that since he had left the bed, she had rolled over and now occupied the place that he had vacated. Even in sleep it seemed that she gravitated to him, as if unconsciously she was drawn to his warmth.

The idea of *her* warmth was seductive. She had held him and enfolded him in a gentle warmth that he was in danger of becoming addicted to. Tonight, even knowing that he had needed to restrain his libido and take things slowly, he'd had trouble controlling himself. If they stayed in bed for a week, he didn't think he would be able to have enough of her.

She loved him.

She hadn't said as much, but Marc couldn't dismiss the knowledge. Even if he hadn't come to that conclusion, he couldn't dismiss the fact that Jenna had never slept with another man, she had only ever been his.

Maybe it was a little primitive and old-fashioned of him to be happy that she had only ever belonged to him, but O'Halloran didn't care. On that point, his feelings were straightforward and uncomplicated and making love had just cemented what he wanted.

If Jenna was prepared to take the risk and give him her love, then he was taking it.

His phone vibrated again.

Backing away from the open door, Marc strolled to his laptop, which was on the coffee table. He flipped open the computer. It was on sleep mode, so the screen saver flicked off and he went straight into his mail program.

With any luck he would be back before it was fully light, but just in case he typed a quick email and pressed the send button.

Leaving the laptop open on the coffee table, he stepped quietly out of the door.

West and Carter were waiting in the lobby. Minutes later, they walked through to the underground parking lot, climbed into Carter's sleek black utility truck and headed towards the southern side of town.

Tell had a street office and owned a house under his own name, which Farrell had under twenty-four-hour surveillance. But West, with his uncanny nose for tax and business scams, had been able to unearth the interesting fact that Tell filtered most of what he earned through some murky trust, which just happened to also own a warehouse at a third address.

It was growing light as they pulled up a block short of the warehouse premises.

Carter stared at the roofline in the distance. "I'm taking it we're not allowed to shoot this guy."

Marc flipped back the lapel of his jacket. "I've got the gun."

Carter waited for West to exit then extracted a duffel, which he slung over one shoulder before locking the truck. "If Tell's got a gun, my wife is not going to be happy. She thinks I'm at a reunion, hanging out at a hotel bar, swapping stories."

West turned his head, as movement registered off to the left. "Just hold that thought and try not to get shot."

A group of joggers appeared out of the mist, most of

them older women with toy dogs on leashes. They were followed by a group of power-walking senior citizens.

Marc checked his watch and began to walk. They passed a sign that announced that they had just entered the Sunnyvale Retirement Village. He studied the surrounding houses. To go with the retirement village theme, they were all similar-sized cottages painted in soft pastel colours. Plantings of petunias were popular.

Carter lifted a hand to an old lady wearing a bright red bandanna who was lagging behind the rest of the power walkers.

A pink cottage with large, painted butterflies adorning the front porch loomed. Marc stepped around a tiny pile of dog droppings that was probably going to get some senior citizen blackballed from the village before the day was out.

His gaze caught on Carter's faded rucksack. "What have you got in the rucksack?"

He snagged it off Carter's shoulder before Carter could protest, although Marc did it carefully. He had heard stories about Rawlings, and quite a few of them had involved explosives, because that had been one of his particular skills in the SAS.

Dragging open the flap, Marc peered inside. There was a lump of what looked like putty wrapped in plastic in the bottom. There was also a separate package that had to contain detonators.

He had told Carter to leave his gun at home. He had just forgotten to rule out fireworks. "Where in hell did you get C4?"

Carter reclaimed the rucksack with barely a flicker. "A friend had it in his garage. He was worried one of the kids would get their hands on it, so he asked me to dispose of it."

Marc moved sideways on the path, giving Carter extra room. "Don't tell me it's past its use-by date."

Carter's expression was scarily neutral. "With any luck, that could be today."

Marc stopped at the neatly hedged rear of a large building that stood cheek by jowl with the butterfly cottage.

Shaded by thick trees and with tightly controlled and manicured shrubs that were clearly tended by the village residents, it could almost pass for a modern barn-style house. In reality, it was the edge of a light industrial area. "This is it."

West surveyed the building. "Looks like a garden center."

Carter stepped into the deep shade of a tree. "Cool. Since we don't have guns, maybe we'll get lucky and find some gardening implements of some kind."

Marc ignored the banter.

There was no guarantee they would find Tell, but he hadn't vanished into thin air. Tell had to be basing himself somewhere in town. If they found him, Marc wasn't about to worry about the legalities of the situation. They would grab him *then* place the call to Farrell.

Tell strolled into the Lombard Hotel dressed in a business suit and carrying a briefcase. He had already made a reservation over the internet, using his new identity, so signing in and picking up his key was just a formality.

He didn't intend to stay. Not very long, anyway.

The room key was just a convenience to get him

up to the concierge floor where, according to one of Jenna Whitmore's most popular fan sites, she was staying the night.

While the fan site had proved a useful resource for tracing Whitmore's movements, it hadn't been able to supply him with the exact number of the room. Although finding it shouldn't be a problem. It would be easy enough to pinpoint the room by the security outside.

He took the lift, checked his room key then strolled slowly down hushed, thickly carpeted corridors. The Lombard Hotel was five-star and swanky—even the air smelled expensive.

He passed a darkly suited security guard. Two doors down, he found his room.

The coincidence that he had been placed so close to Whitmore made up for the inconvenience of having to pay the exorbitant price for the room.

Checking his watch, he stepped inside, closed the door behind him then, with quick deft movements, unpacked and assembled the 9mm Browning he had tucked into his briefcase. A handgun he had chosen specifically because it had originally been designed for the military, the Browning was a thing of beauty.

Walking through to the bathroom, he glued on a fake moustache, and fitted in contacts that changed the colour of his irises from light blue to brown. When his eyes had stopped watering, he slipped on a pair of glasses that had a faint tint, enough to distract anyone who took a second look at him.

A thrill shot down his spine as he slid the gun into the shoulder holster he was wearing and surveyed the effect in the mirror.

According to Whitmore's schedule, she would be leaving the hotel to catch an early flight south just after breakfast.

She wasn't ever going to make that flight.

Sunlight flowing across the bed woke Jenna. Rolling over, she discovered that she was alone and from the coldness of O'Halloran's side, he had been gone for some time.

The faint stiffness of various muscles and the definite feeling of tenderness between her thighs sent hot memory flashing through her. They had made love three times, the third time sleepy and prolonged and intense as they'd lain in the dark, almost more content to hold each other than move. In those long, drawn-out moments it had been easy to imagine that O'Halloran really did love her, that what they had would magically metamorphose into a real relationship.

Stepping out of bed she searched for something to wear and settled on one of O'Halloran's business shirts, which was still folded neatly in his suitcase. White and crisp with a thin blue line, it was clean but it still had the subtle, stomach-clenching smell of O'Halloran.

Maybe it was a cliché to wear it. She didn't care. She was still high on the humming delight of having spent an entire night in bed with her man, and she was determined to wallow in the experience while she could.

Hugging the shirt close to her skin, she strolled to the bathroom, refusing to think about an end to her time with O'Halloran. As she stripped off, she glimpsed herself in the vanity mirror. Her hair was a languorous tangle, her mouth pale and swollen, a faint red mark decorated the side of her neck where O'Halloran's jaw had scraped her tender skin.

What they'd done together was imprinted all over her and, in that moment, she knew that no matter how modern or independent she strived to be, in her heart all she wanted was a life with O'Halloran. She was in love with him and the emotional risk was huge.

If she couldn't have him, she already knew that she wouldn't have anyone else. She wouldn't ever get married and, unless she could achieve a solo adoption, she would never have the family she craved.

She didn't know why O'Halloran had touched her so deeply. It was a fact that they had never ended up spending that much time together. She knew more about most of her casual friends than she did about O'Halloran.

Maybe it was simply that she had been so vulnerable when she had met him, or because when she had ended the original relationship she had still been in love with him and had never gotten closure.

Whatever the reason, at some deep, bedrock level, a stubborn part of her had taken one look at O'Halloran and chosen him.

After showering, she quickly changed into a business suit, because she would have to leave to catch her flight straight after breakfast.

She checked her watch and frowned. She had assumed O'Halloran had gone down to breakfast early, but if that was the case, he would have been back by now.

Frowning when she remembered she didn't have her phone, she walked out to the lounge and quickly checked her email.

A long list of social networking prompts flowed in with regular emails. She ran her eye casually down the list, automatically designating everything as non-urgent until her gaze snagged on Lydell88.

An automatic warm glow flowed through her. Lydell must have read her book.

She checked her watch. She had a few minutes before she needed to go down for breakfast.

When she opened up the email, the message was simple and succinct. Check the mail program on the laptop next to yours.

She frowned, briefly confused. Although there was only one logical reason for Lydell to know that there was a laptop sitting side by side with hers on the coffee table.

Taking a deep breath and feeling suddenly shaky, she bent down and activated the touch pad of O'Halloran's laptop. It flashed off sleep mode and she found herself staring at O'Halloran's mail program, which was already open.

And which also happened to be Lydell88's mail program.

Legs feeling a little wobbly, she sat down on the couch and simply stared at the file of emails that O'Halloran had left open for her to see. Tears burned her eyes, trickled down her cheeks.

She had emailed Lydell88 for years, slowly nurturing the building friendship with him. She had been careful. She hadn't wanted to impose or ask more than he'd wanted to give. From the careful way he'd never allowed the online friendship to cross over into a real personal relationship, even though they both lived in Auckland, she'd known that he was wary of intimacy.

She'd respected his need for distance, but it was a fact that most of the correspondence had been instigated by him. Sometimes, on rare occasions, they had even chatted on live forums she had hosted then afterward continued on into the night on her website chat line.

The conversations had never gotten too personal, but in an odd way they had become her emotional lifeline because underneath the police procedural information and the technicalities of plot, she had been aware that Lydell88 *cared.* In a quiet low-key way, he had been the closest thing she'd had to a relationship in years.

She wiped tears from her cheeks, careful not to smudge her mascara, and found herself grinning like a loon as she began opening and reading the emails *O'Halloran* had sent to her.

Her heart pounded as she stopped reading and scrolled down the file, trying to count how many, like a miser gleefully counting dollar bills. There were literally hundreds.

O'Halloran read her books. He *liked* them.

Dazed, she reflected that it was no wonder she had fallen in love with him, because he really was perfect for her.

Outside in the corridor she registered the rattle of a room-service trolley. A knock on the door distracted her from her all-important tally.

Still feeling like dancing a jig because she was so happy, Jenna answered the door, drawn by the only thing that could drag her away from O'Halloran's entrancing laptop: the possibility that it could be the man himself.

The door swung open and was immediately jammed by the trolley she'd heard out in the hall.

A tall, suited guy, who looked nothing like the bodyguard O'Halloran had introduced her to last night, pointed a large handgun at her head.

"Good morning, Jenna." He shoved the trolley, forcing her back into the room as he kicked the door shut behind him.

Jenna stared at the glinting glasses and what was obviously a fake moustache. He looked different, his eyes were dark, not light, but she would know him anywhere. "Branden Tell."

"That's right. Not the hero, the villain."

Chapter 16

Sunlight beamed through chinks in the dusty little room Branden Tell had dragged her into, shortly before taping her to a chair, taping her mouth and leaving.

She knew he hadn't gone far, because periodically she could hear a soft tapping sound, as if he was typing, and once she had heard him speak on the phone.

She had strained to hear what he was saying, but his voice had been too muffled, indicating that there was at least another room separating them.

That suited her just fine; she didn't want him close. Long minutes of being clamped against his side while he'd urged her into a service elevator, the barrel of the gun digging into her side, had been enough. Nine years ago she hadn't particularly liked Tell. Now she definitely didn't like him.

Rocking the chair slightly, trying to make as little

noise as possible, she managed to shimmy around in a painful circle, so she could get a good look at her surroundings.

Not inspiring. A concrete floor and one corrugated iron wall through which tiny beams of sunlight glowed. The only positive was that there was a nail sticking out of one of the timbers. It wasn't much to pin her hopes on, but the rusty old nail, combined with the fact that Branden had only taped her wrists, not tied them, provided some hope.

That, and the fact that Branden had made her chew sleeping pills, thinking they would knock her out.

The pills, depending on which one—and she had tried them all—did make her drowsy, but the effect never lasted long. Her doctor had given up prescribing them for her occasional insomniac episodes, because usually half an hour after taking one she was as wide-awake as ever.

From the bitter taste in her mouth, the dull headache and general feeling of lethargy, she concluded that Tell had given her one of the stronger formulations. Although that had been a good hour ago now. Tied up in the back of a military-style Hummer, she had fought the drowsy effect of the pill in an effort to see exactly where Tell was taking her. Although every time he had checked on her she had played dead for him.

She had decided that if he thought she was unconscious then that was an advantage of a sort. Given that she was pretty sure Tell didn't mean her to live, she needed to exploit every advantage if she was to have any hope of escape.

She had timed the drive, which had been a good forty minutes, and she knew from overhead signs she'd glimpsed that they had been on the Southern motorway. The change from the roar of motorway traffic to sporadic passing vehicles signalled that Tell had turned off into one of the suburbs south of Auckland.

Working the chair until she was backed up to the nail, she tried to catch the edge of the tape on the nail head. The process was awkward, because she couldn't see what she was doing and had to work by feel. Added to that her hands were starting to go numb, which meant she had to work quickly. If they went completely numb she wouldn't be able to feel where the nail head was.

After the first few minutes her shoulders and arms began to burn, but she gritted her teeth and kept rubbing the tape back and forth on the nail. Every now and then she slipped and the nail scraped over her skin, but she ignored the discomfort.

Stopping to rest her shoulder muscles, which were starting to cramp, she tried pulling her wrists apart. Before there hadn't been any movement, now there was enough flexibility that she could wiggle her wrists a little. It was definitely working because feeling was pouring back into her hands in the form of fiery pins and needles.

Jaw gritted, she started the sawing process again. Time crawled by. Her shoulders and back ached and the effort made her break out in a sweat. Her wrists and hands felt like they were on fire, but she was eventually rewarded with a sudden loosening.

In the distance she heard a rumble, as if a large roller door had been activated, and the sound of a heavy truck. Abruptly, the sporadic sound of vehicles fell into its context. She wasn't hearing road noise. The building must be part of an industrial area somewhere.

If it was a warehouse of some kind that meant it would be one of many. So there had to be people nearby, and they were probably ridiculously close. All she had to do was get free and find some way to sneak past Tell.

The heavy detonation of an explosion jerked her head up, followed by the rending shriek of metal, so close it hurt her ears. She could hear footsteps.

Heart pounding so hard she could barely breathe, eyes wide, she stared at the shadows that filled the doorway, hope and a fierce exultation filling her.

O'Halloran.

She knew it. He had come to get her.

O'Halloran stepped through the twisted ruin of the door Carter had just blown off its hinges into the cavernous space of the warehouse.

Carter and West flowed in behind him. Moving quickly, they checked the series of storerooms that opened off the main area.

Kicking open the final door, O'Halloran stared into an empty room. The place was dusty and the only footprints were theirs. Tell hadn't been here for weeks, if not months.

Knowledge nagged at the back of his mind. He had made the mistake of remembering Tell as he had been years ago, an unassuming student, and not overly bright. But Tell had been smart enough to elude Farrell, and Marc couldn't forget that he had kept *him* on a string for six years.

West walked up behind him. "He's not here."

O'Halloran holstered his gun and checked his watch. "Nope, he's somewhere else."

Now that they'd exhausted this avenue he needed

to get back to the hotel, because Jenna had a flight to catch. Farrell had a watch on the airports and Tell's house and an APB out on Tell's vehicle, which apparently was a Hummer.

A shadow falling across the sunny entrance to the warehouse made Marc stiffen. An elderly man was poking his walking stick at the remains of the door.

He fixed Carter with a beady eye. "This doesn't belong to that crook Morrison, or his son. We made him an offer he couldn't refuse. It now belongs to the Retirement Village Trust, as of last week. Planning on turning it into a community hall."

Carter had the grace to look guilty. "Uh, sorry about that—"

"I hope you're going to fix the door."

"Sure, I've got tools in the truck. Will tomorrow do?"

"It will, and don't think about weaselling out of the job. We've got your licence tag and security footage. The neighbourhood watch is on the ball around here."

Marc's attention sharpened. "Morrison? Was that the cop?"

"That's right. Got indicted for extorting money from organized crime figures and gangs."

"I remember." He should. He had made the arrest and filed the charges.

As they walked back to Carter's truck, disparate pieces of information began to fall into place. Tell had been illegitimate, but he had let it be known that his father was a cop, which was why he had wanted to follow him either into the military or the police force.

The same year Natalie had died, Marc had prosecuted a crooked cop by the name of Branden Morrison.

Sliding his phone out of his pocket, he short-dialled

Farrell. A few minutes later, she called back, confirming that Morrison was Tell's father.

His stomach tensed at the implications as he swung into the passenger seat of Carter's truck. He had been looking for motivation and a way to tie Tell into both Natalie's and Jared's deaths and Jenna's stalking. He had thought it had to be Tell's fascination with Natalie, the added resentment that Marc had the career that Tell had been shooting for, combined with his fear that Jenna's book might expose his crime.

The only problem with that scenario was, why risk exposure by going after Jenna now, when it was too late to stop the book being published anyway?

It would have been far better if Tell had stayed quiet and let the whole thing fade. After all, the book was fiction. As closely involved as Marc was, he had read it and not connected the dots.

Tell could have quietly sold up all of his assets, emigrated and dodged possible charges, but he hadn't; he'd stayed because he'd always had another, ultimately more powerful motive: revenge.

The yearly emails from Tell were the clincher. He had never had any intention of fading into the background. All Jenna's book had done was present him with another platform to act out that revenge.

The link that strung Tell's crimes together was simple: it was him.

Marc stared out of the window at the heavy morning traffic on the motorway—rush hour was getting underway.

Checking his watch, he tried phoning the hotel room again, then Dawson's phone. He frowned. Jenna should have picked up, she would be anxious to leave, and should have phoned him by now. Something was wrong.

Before he could dial Blade's cell, his phone vibrated again.

It was Blade. Dawson was down, with a concussion, and Jenna was missing. He had checked security tapes and found the footage. A tall guy dressed like a bodyguard had taken her down a service elevator into the underground garage. The guy had looked nondescript apart from a moustache, which had obviously been fake, but he had been driving a military-style Hummer.

Chest tight, heart hammering, Marc hung up. He stared blankly ahead, no longer seeing the interior of the truck or the cars and buildings flashing by. Grimly, he tried to think.

He could second-guess Tell, he'd done it often enough with other criminals. All it took was careful analysis, but for long seconds all he could think about was the way Jenna had trusted him last night. The moment this morning when he had watched her roll over in bed and reach for him. And he hadn't been there.

In that moment he realised, too late, that he wanted to be there for her—personally, professionally, every way there was.

The enormity of the mistake he had made in going after Tell instead of leaving the enforcement work to Farrell sank in a little deeper.

For long seconds, he was flung further back into the past, to a burning building and a wife and child who had needed him. He hadn't been there for Natalie and Jared.

Knowing that Tell had murdered them had made a difference. Looking back, there was no way he could have known his arrest of Morrison would have a backlash. Tell would have staked out the house. With Natalie keeping her correspondence with him secret, Marc had been cut out of the loop, literally.

But that wasn't the case with Jenna. She had shared everything with him: her fear and distress, her passion and love.

His fingers closed into fists. She had even helped him with the investigation.

Natalie and Jared's loss still hurt, but he'd had years to come to terms with it. But the prospect of losing Jenna filled him with desperate fear.

In her quiet way, Jenna was his, more intimately and completely than any other woman had ever been. Over the years, he had gotten to know every nook and cranny of her mind, her quirky humour, the softness of her emotions, the steely way she had refused to allow any guy to rush her into bed unless *she* wanted to go there.

And she hadn't. Instead, she had saved herself for him.

He would get her back.

He had to. He loved her.

The realisation hit him like a kick in the chest.

It explained why he had never been able to forget Jenna, even down to emailing her under an alias so even if it was only in a small way, he could continue to be part of her life.

Carter glanced at him and softly swore. "What's happened?"

Keeping his voice toneless, Marc related the bare details Blade had given him.

Carter pulled over. "What do you want to do?"

"Blade's already called Farrell. She's put an APB

out on Tell. He's driving a Hummer, so he should be easy to spot."

The military fetish fitted. Unfortunately, a whole lot of things fitted, now that it was too late.

Too late. The words haunted Marc. Six years ago he had been too late for Natalie and Jared.

He had no intention of being too late for Jenna.

Grabbing his briefcase, he flipped it open and dug out his iPad. Using the software that West had supplied, he checked to see if coordinates for Jenna's phone had been recorded. The result was still negative.

He would keep checking, but time was passing. If Tell had intended to turn on the phone, he would have done it by now. Chances were, he had tossed it.

Marc flicked back to his server and typed in Google. "Tell has another bolt-hole. We just have to find it. His father extorted a lot of money from organized crime figures, which could never be recovered because he tied it up in family trusts. The trusts owned a number of properties. All we have to do is search for property holdings under the name Morrison."

The hits were numerous. A lot of people had been outraged by Morrison's greed. Within seconds, O'Halloran found what he wanted in a sensationalised press offering that had completely ignored the idea of confidentiality and had published a list of Morrison's assets.

With a sense of disbelief, he noted that there was also an exposé on Morrison's illegitimate children, three at last count, including Branden Tell. Now wasn't a good time to reflect that if he had read the Sunday papers six years ago, he could have solved the case.

He wrote down the addresses of a number of properties in South Auckland, all of which sounded industrial.

Picking up his phone, he called Farrell. She agreed to dispatch cars to check out the addresses he had given her, but at present, thanks to the arson investigation, she had limited manpower.

Jaw locked, Marc gave Carter the nearest address. It was a long shot, but they had to start somewhere. He had a cold itch up his spine. Time was important.

He needed to find Tell before the man had time to put the next part of his plan into action.

And Marc was convinced that Tell had something planned. Otherwise, why bother to kidnap Jenna?

If Tell had wanted to extract a simple, straightforward revenge he could have obtained that by shooting Jenna in their hotel room.

Chapter 17

Jenna's hopes plunged as Tell, not O'Halloran, stepped through the door of her dark little cave of a room. Without the moustache or the glasses, but dressed neatly in a suit, he was all too familiar, shoving her back to the past.

Back to the night of the ball, when Tell had been her escort and she had almost been run down in the dark. Back to just days ago, the chilling replay in the mall parking lot.

Fury poured through her. It had been Tell behind the wheel each time. Of course it had been; the wonder of it was that she hadn't managed to see it before now. As a suspense writer she was used to drawing together disparate pieces of information, looking for patterns, she just hadn't been capable of doing it with her own life.

If she could have spoken, she would have coldly

stated that she knew exactly what he was, what he had done not just to her and her family, but to O'Halloran, but all that came out was a strangled, muffled sound.

Tell frowned. "Damn, you're awake. Not that it matters. It'll only make the show more interesting."

He cocked his head to one side as if listening for her reply, then grinned. "Sorry, forgot you can't talk. Bet that must be a novelty."

He moved forward with a deceptively fast, gliding step that made her heart freeze. She thought he was going to hit her, but instead he ripped the tape off. "Although, I guess as a writer you're more concerned with writing trashy novels than talking to actual people, which would be why you've never managed to find anyone."

Jenna gasped at the burn across her mouth from the tape. She didn't think he had actually taken any skin off, it just felt like it.

Forcing herself to ignore Tell's jab about her personal life, and the chilling knowledge that he had obviously kept tabs on her over the years, she sucked in a lungful of stale air and slumped a little, as if the defiance she'd just shown had exhausted her and she was fighting sleep. "If you don't like books, don't read."

"Good advice."

He stared at her and frowned. Adrenaline surged through her as he continued to stand over her. He hadn't seemed to have noticed that she had moved the chair, but if he did, it wouldn't take him long to put two and two together and check her wrists.

Another rill of panic shot through her as he bent down, but he didn't check her wrists, he simply picked up the chair with her in it.

Jenna's stomach lurched as he carried her, although she was more concerned that he might notice she had practically sawed through the tape binding her wrists.

Seconds later, he set the chair down by a stack of cartons in what looked like the main room of a warehouse. A bare, iron roof soared overhead. The Hummer he'd used to transport her here was now parked inside and occupied one end of the room. Boxes of varying shapes and sizes were stacked at the other end.

Jenna's blood ran cold when she noted the contents: security systems.

The connection she had made when she'd been half-asleep the previous night had been heart-poundingly correct. Hope surged afresh, sending blood pounding through her veins, burning through the dull, heavy lethargy the pills had induced.

O'Halloran had taken her suggestion that Tell could be linked somehow with security systems rather than firms seriously enough that he had gotten out of bed and started making calls. He had come back to bed, but left in the early hours. The conclusion was obvious; he had a lead on Tell.

He would be searching. She knew better than anyone what O'Halloran was like. He was dogged, relentless. If anyone could find her, he would.

Letting herself sag a little farther in the chair as if she was fighting the effects of the sleeping pills Tell had given her, she continued to take stock of her surroundings.

There was a desk neatly piled with papers and what looked like order books. An expensive laptop sat next to a printer and modem and other various pieces of office paraphernalia.

Her gaze snagged on the sleek shape of a stylish white phone. *Her phone.*

She jerked her gaze away in case Tell noticed that she'd spotted it, but she needn't have bothered. He was busy loading a stack of folders and boxes into the back of his Hummer.

Getting ready to leave.

Taking a deep breath, she forced her wrists apart as far as they'd go. Frustratingly, the tape had stretched, but hadn't broken. Closing her eyes, she sent up a desperate prayer. She needed help, and she needed it soon.

She needed Tell to leave the room for one minute, two at the most. She was pretty sure she had enough stretch in the tape that she could shimmy out of the chair, get over to the desk and switch on her phone.

Long minutes passed while Tell continued to load the Hummer. The soft burr of a phone saw him straightening. He answered his cell, a call that seemed to be about flight details, then had to set the phone down while he searched for a file he must have stacked in the backseat of the Hummer.

Another loud detonation made her jump. From the rending sound of metal being crushed, she guessed that the building was cheek by jowl with a car-recycling plant.

Tell was busy, with his back to her, and there was enough sound that he wouldn't hear the noise she was bound to make getting loose from the chair. She would never have a better chance.

Giving the tape around her wrists a final stretch, she planted her feet firmly apart on the concrete floor, braced herself and pushed upward. She managed to slide her arms and wrists up a few inches, then, in order to clear the top of the chair, she had to shimmy and straighten by increments. In the process, the chair wobbled and banged on the concrete.

Adrenaline flowing, she darted a glance at Tell, who was still rummaging in the backseat of the Hummer, as she pulled hard at the tape. It had stretched enough that she could step backwards through the loop of her arms. She was still tied, but now at least her hands were in front.

Walking quickly to the desk, she picked up the phone and depressed the start button. She had a moment to wonder if Murphy's Law had struck and the battery was flat, then it activated with a soft glow and a faint musical chime.

She debated making a run for it with the phone, but the distance to the door was a good fifteen meters. Tell would catch her before she could reach it.

Her priority had to be ensuring that the GPS search program had enough time to connect with her phone and download her location. Working quickly, she scrolled through to settings and turned off all of the noises the phone made. Setting the phone back on the desk, she placed an invoice book on top of it to hide the faint glow that signalled it was on.

Just as she was about to return to her chair she saw the small squat shape of a box-cutter blade.

A sharp thunk signalled that Tell had shut the door of the Hummer. Her heart slamming hard in her chest, Jenna snatched up the box cutter and covered the four paces to her chair. She sat down a split second before Tell half turned to check on her, a document in one hand, phone to his ear.

He stared at her then looked away. Jenna went limp

as a noodle. The box cutter was hidden in the folds of her skirt, and he hadn't noticed that her hands were tied in the front, not the back.

Working quickly, she slit the tape, wedged the box cutter between the small of her back and the seat then clasped her hands together behind the chair as if they were tied.

Tell's laptop pinged, indicating he had mail. He hung up from his call and strolled past her to his desk. Apart from raking a cold glance over her, he barely seemed to notice she was there.

He refreshed the screen then muttered a hard, sharp word. "Damn, how did he manage to find my email address?"

Attention riveted, Jenna stared at the laptop screen as Tell scrolled down. The email appeared to be blank.

Frowning, he opened up the attachment that had come with the email. A photograph of Jenna opened up, filling the entire screen.

Cursing beneath his breath, Tell hit the delete button. The photo and the email winked out as he slammed the laptop shut, but it was too late, she'd already seen it.

He might have emailed Tell, but the message had been for her.

Fierce satisfaction filled her, although she kept her expression carefully blank. The email informed her that O'Halloran had gone through Tell's life with a fine-tooth comb and had found his business email address. When it came to research and investigative method, O'Halloran was clinical and focused. By now, what he didn't know about Tell wouldn't fit on a postage stamp.

Tears filled Jenna's eyes and made her feel shaky inside. For O'Halloran to have sent the email at that moment meant he must have been monitoring the GPS program on her phone. He couldn't know who had turned on the phone and he hadn't risked calling her number, because if Tell had been using the phone, that would have alerted him. Instead, he had put a call through to her in the only way he safely could, by emailing Tell.

He had the coordinates, which meant he was on his way. She didn't know how long she had to wait, but at a guess based on the time it had taken Tell to drive here, it would be half an hour or so.

Her chest squeezed tight. The photograph O'Halloran had used was an old one, nine years old to be exact. She remembered when it had been taken, during a carefree, impromptu picnic at the beach.

Despite the fact that O'Halloran would be working hard and literally have no time, he had somehow managed to find a photo of her from the time they had dated and send it out into cyberspace.

It had been a crazy, quixotic, *romantic* gesture. There was no guarantee that Tell would have even accessed his email. Even if he had, the chances were that she wouldn't be in a position to see the photograph, but still, he'd sent it. And in that moment she saw another side to O'Halloran.

He was in turns frustrating and uncomplicatedly, ruthlessly male. He was her lover, friend and protector. Most importantly, he was *hers*.

The concept settled in, filling her with a fierce sense of certainty.

O'Halloran hadn't ever given her any words of love. When it came to emotional discussions, he was the original Sphinx, but that didn't matter. He was hers in all the ways that mattered. Maybe it would take him a little time to get around to telling her. That was fine; she could wait.

All she had to do was get out of this alive.

Tell checked his watch then walked back in the direction of the Hummer to make another call. The sound of a large truck backing up to the roller door stopped him in his tracks.

Tell spun. Instead of going to the door, he picked up a can, unscrewed the lid and tossed it away as he walked toward her.

Horror filled Jenna as he began dousing the stacked boxes next to her with gasoline.

Marc and members of the Special Tactics Squad he used to command fanned out like dark shadows, flowing around the warehouse to key entry points: a rear window, a side door and either side of the main roller door. Seconds later they were all in position.

Cornell, the senior detective at Auckland Central, hadn't been happy about Marc's insistence that he be included in the team, but in this instance he'd allowed it because Marc knew Tell, and he'd also added the condition that he couldn't personally shoot anyone.

Marc hadn't made that promise, and Cornell hadn't pressed the point. He knew what Marc had lost at the hands of Tell better than anyone.

Marc spoke into a lip mike. Carter and West had driven the large delivery truck, which was presently parked hard up against the roller door of the warehouse. If Tell tried to escape, he'd find that avenue blocked.

There was a moment of quiet, until the team sniper indicated that he was in position.

O'Halloran gave the order to proceed. In the same instant, he smelled smoke.

Panic gripped him, the kind of icy, bone-deep dread that had hit him six years ago when he'd arrived home to find his house ablaze.

He smashed the rear window and climbed through into a dark room that was already filling with smoke. A second team member, a young ultra-fit officer called Trent who was relatively new to the squad, followed a half step behind, covering him.

Glock held in a two-handed grip, Marc stepped through an open door into a corridor. He checked what looked like an empty storage room and kept moving. When he saw the leap of flames, he roared Jenna's name.

Sucking in a lungful of smoky air he called again.

The sound of a vehicle filled the air as he stepped into a room that was rapidly turning into a blazing inferno. Flames and black smoke poured from a central pyre, licking up the walls.

Someone said his name, the sound hoarse. A split second later, Jenna loomed out of the smoke.

Marc grabbed her, one arm snaking around her waist and hauling her in tight against him as he dragged her and half carried her back the way he'd come. Seconds later the Hummer, engine screaming, smashed through the far wall of the warehouse.

Marc had a moment to haul Jenna in against the wall of his chest and wrap both arms around her before the sudden gush of fresh air sent flames whooshing.

Heat singed Marc's skin even through the fire-retardant overalls, which were standard issue, and the body armour he was wearing. Coughing, eyes running, he swung Jenna into his arms. Almost totally blinded by the smoke, he found the room where he'd entered the warehouse by following the draught of air flowing from the window.

He handed Jenna through the window, then clambered after her. Seconds later, they were outside on the cool green grass, the blue sky arching above, cloudless except for the pall of smoke that funnelled up from the burning warehouse.

When he could breathe without coughing, Marc studied the burning building, a sight he profoundly hoped that he would never see again.

"Are you all right?"

Jenna's hand linked with his. He looked into her concerned gaze and his heart locked up.

He didn't know how, but she knew what the fire made him feel, the memories that seared him and the grief that should have made him drop dead in his tracks. But it hadn't, he had kept breathing, kept living. Life moved on and now he was happy that it had.

He cupped her face, which was pink from the heat, and sooty. It didn't matter, Jenna had always been beautiful to him. "I love you."

She smiled, tears tracking down her cheeks. "I know. Thank you for the emails, Lydell88."

He found himself smiling into her eyes. The email correspondence had started out as a way to keep tabs on Jenna and make sure she was okay. He had never intended for it to develop into anything more, but somehow the exchanges had metamorphosed into an addictive habit he'd had a hard time controlling. "I wasn't sure if you had time to find them."

"I'm glad I did. It kept me going after Tell busted into the hotel room." Reaching up, she slid her fingers into his hair. Cupping his skull, she gently pulled his head down until his forehead settled on hers. "I love you, too, and have for a long time now."

Going up on her toes, she sealed the words with a kiss that was soft and gentle and filled with the kind of promise he thought he'd given up on a long time ago.

She eased back a few inches. "Don't you want to go after Tell?"

He rubbed his thumbs across her cheeks, wiping away the tears. "Nope."

The relief in Jenna's gaze made his heart squeeze tight. In that moment, he made a second vow. From now on, Jenna came first. Happily, he had enough money that he could afford to follow McCabe's example; the business could go hang.

She smiled. "Good, because I think your friend Carter took care of that. I don't know if you've noticed, but he kind of ran over Tell with that truck."

Jenna strolled over to the two vehicles with O'Halloran, happily leaning into his side and enjoying the feel of his arm clamped possessively around her waist. She was barefoot, bruised and scraped, her hair was singed and she looked like a chimney sweep, but she was almost dizzy with happiness.

In the oddball way that it worked, her writer's mind threw up a question about the past that had been niggling at her off and on. "Just one thing. When, exactly, after we first broke up did you visit the air base to find out about my family background?"

"And Dane Hawkins."

She drew in a sharp breath at the sudden visual of Dane: warm brown eyes, brown hair shot with surfieblond streaks. But like the sepia-toned photographs lining her stairwell, the image now seemed faded and distant, a pleasant memory rather than a wrenching one. "And Dane."

"A couple of days after we broke up. Why do you think I was worried enough to follow you when you left Tell at the ball that night and walked home alone?"

She gripped the lapels of his overalls. Her eyes were burning with tears again, her chest squeezed tight. She couldn't help it, she felt like she'd just stepped out of a dark tunnel into blinding sunlight. "So you knew what had happened before we made love."

Again it hit her. That was why he had been so silent and withdrawn, and why he had let her go with barely a word. Not because he didn't care, but because he did.

His gaze was dark and impossibly soft. "I knew you didn't want the relationship because I was a cop. Up until then the way you were hadn't made sense because I knew you wanted me." His hands curled around her arms, pulled her close. "We shouldn't have made love. I shouldn't have touched you, but the near accident pushed things over the edge. And," he admitted, "I hoped that if I made love to you it might be enough for you to leave the grief behind."

And choose him.

Coiling her arms around his neck, Jenna answered the question in his eyes, the one question she knew he wouldn't be able to ask. "Dane had been gone for almost two years when you first asked me out. I knew you were a cop, and still I agreed, which should tell you something. I wasn't ready for a relationship with anybody, most especially a soldier or a cop, but it was a fact that I couldn't resist you. That night we made love, Dane didn't come into the equation."

Relief flared in his gaze. "That's why I didn't come near you again, until I started dating Natalie."

"And then Nat was a good friend. Trust me, I know. After I lost Dane, I wouldn't have gotten through it without her."

His forehead dropped on hers. "Did I tell you that I loved you?"

She couldn't stop smiling. O'Halloran loved her. He had always loved her. She knew he had loved Natalie and Jared, too, and that they would always have a special place in his heart. But, like her time with Dane, that part of his life had come to an end and couldn't be gotten back.

Now that they had found each other for the second time, the future stretched forward, almost unbearably bright. It seemed almost impossibly greedy, that after nine years of waiting she could finally have the man she loved with all her heart, and the family and life she craved.

Marc kept Jenna close as he joined the members of the STS, who were gathered around the truck and the Hummer, lethal automatics held, barrels pointing to the ground. Like him, they were all, except for the sniper who had been holed up on a roof across the road, singed and covered with soot.

In the distance, sirens wailed. The fire trucks were on their way. Not that there would be much for them to do by the time they got here. The warehouse was little more than a shell and was already close to totalled.

Marc lifted a brow at Carter as he checked out the

odd configuration of the two vehicles. "How did you get the Hummer wedged underneath like that?"

Carter leaned against the truck, which Marc had borrowed from one of their security suppliers and which he was now going to have to pay to have repaired.

He didn't care. He had more money than he needed, and if Carter hadn't pulled the stunt with the truck, Tell might have gotten away. Hummers were notoriously difficult to stop. Using the truck to cut him off had been a one-shot chance, and it had paid off.

Carter had an innocent look on his face, which, for a hardened former SAS assault specialist, was difficult to achieve. "It's all a bit confusing now, what with the smoke and everything—"

"It's not an insurance job. I'm paying."

"Cool. Then I drove him down."

A cop cruiser pulled in at the curb. Farrell and Hansen climbed out. Marc grinned when he noticed Farrell was driving.

He checked in the cab. Tell was pinned by the steering wheel and crumpled metal. Stuck like a sardine in a can, he was conscious and definitely unhappy.

West braced a hand on the Hummer and peered in. "I guess we should call an ambulance."

Carter shrugged. "I'm thinking we should run it past Farrell first. She won't be happy if we make a decision without her."

West nodded. "That is absolutely right. We should wait."

Farrell put the cell she had been talking into in her pocket as she came to a halt by the wreck of the Hummer. Hansen strolled around the vehicle and checked out Tell. "Looks like we won't need the cuffs. Shame, I was looking forward to the moment."

Farrell dug in her pocket and handed Marc a sheet of paper. "That little ritual was reserved for O'Halloran, anyway. But maybe if you talk to the firemen nicely, they'll give you a turn with the Jaws of Life." She shot Marc a look that, for Farrell, who was the ultimate professional, was oddly soft. "Hey, good job."

Marc studied the sheet, which was a list of more than twenty unsolved crimes.

Farrell smiled grimly. "Recognize some of those? We worked a few together. I ran a list of crimes using the security system as the common denominator, like you suggested, and bingo. Our mystery burglar turned out to be Tell. At current estimates, he's stolen more than a million dollars' worth of high-end appliances, cash and fine jewellery."

"Murder, attempted murder, burglary and arson." Satisfaction took some of the edge off the anger that had burned through him when he had realized that Tell was the perpetrator. "With any luck, by the time he gets out, he'll be an old man. Did you realize his father was Morrison?"

He saw the moment Farrell put it all together. "So that's why he went for you. You put his father away."

Marc tightened his hold on Jenna, her warmth and softness reminding him of the single most important fact. She was safe, and she was his. "Except he couldn't quite bring himself to attack me directly, instead he attacked the women in my life."

"A coward." Farrell smiled coldly at Hansen, who had straightened from checking on Tell's condition, and who now had his phone out. "Hansen, make that a big wait on the ambulance."

Epilogue

The wedding was held in the little church just down the road from Jenna's house. Old and beautifully kept, with soaring stained-glass windows, the church was big enough to hold all of Marc's and Jenna's families and friends.

McCabe, Blade Lombard and West and Carter were there, along with their wives and families. Elaine Farrell had also accepted the invitation, along with her partner, a sleek well-groomed businessman.

The ceremony was traditional; the bride wore white. As Marc slipped the ring on her finger and Jenna, in turn, placed a ring on his, the vows they made echoed softly.

Minutes later, Jenna caught the misty smile on her Aunt Mary's face. As she and Marc walked into the vestry to sign the register, a fine tension she had barely been aware of dissolved. Aunt Mary was intensely maternal. Jenna knew she had found it hard to let go of each and every one of her children. She knew Aunt Mary loved her as if she were her own, but that she also loved both Natalie and Jared with a fierce devotion.

The week before the wedding, Mary had invited both Jenna and Marc over for lunch then, out of the blue, she had suggested a visit to the cemetery. The few minutes at the gravesite had been difficult and emotional, but now Jenna understood what Mary had done. There had been no wreath, no soft toy, just a simple bunch of flowers, which she had combined with Marc and Jenna's offering in the little stone vase off to one side.

She had let Natalie and the baby go.

When the signatures were done, and while they waited for their witnesses—McCabe and Jenna's editor, Rachel—to sign, Marc pulled her close. "Are you all right? You look a little pale."

Jenna smiled into his dark eyes, her own misty. "Never better."

And to improve on what had so far been the most sublime day of her life, she reached into the tiny pocket she'd gotten the seamstress to sew into her dress at the last minute and extracted a small blue object. "I have a gift for you."

She handed the baby rattle to Marc. For a split second, his expression was perfectly blank then his piercing gaze shot to hers. "Are you sure?"

"Positive."

With a whoop, Marc swung her into his arms then finally, achingly, he kissed her. From the hubbub of noise and a series of frantic motorised clicks Jenna was dimly aware that some of their guests had crowded into the vestry and the wedding photographer was capturing every angle of their private moment. She didn't care.

Somehow they had come full circle and she was back exactly where she wanted to be, in O'Halloran's arms.

* * * * *

#1735 COWBOY WITH A CAUSE • *Cowboy Café*
by Carla Cassidy

When rancher Adam Benson rents a room from the
wheelchair-bound Melanie Brooks, it doesn't take long
for passion to flare and danger to move in.

#1736 A WIDOW'S GUILTY SECRET

Vengeance in Texas • by Marie Ferrarella

A lonely widow with a newborn falls for the detective
investigating her husband's murder and discovers she has
some very ruthless enemies....

#1737 DEADLY SIGHT • *Code X*
by Cindy Dees

Sent to the National Radio Quiet Zone to investigate...
something...Grayson and Sammie Jo find themselves
fighting for their lives—and falling in love—in the midst of
a dangerous conspiracy.

#1738 GUARDING THE PRINCESS • *Sahara Kings*
by Loreth Anne White

Opposites clash when gruff ex-mercenary Brandt Stryker
sets out to save a glamorous princess from bloodthirsty
bandits in the African bush.

REQUEST YOUR FREE BOOKS!
2 FREE NOVELS PLUS 2 FREE GIFTS!

ROMANTIC
SUSPENSE

Sparked by Danger, Fueled by Passion.

YES! Please send me 2 FREE Harlequin® Romantic Suspense novels and my 2 FREE gifts (gifts are worth about $10). After receiving them, if I don't wish to receive any more books, I can return the shipping statement marked "cancel." If I don't cancel, I will receive 4 brand-new novels every month and be billed just $4.49 per book in the U.S. or $5.24 per book in Canada. That's a saving of at least 14% off the cover price! It's quite a bargain! Shipping and handling is just 50¢ per book in the U.S. and 75¢ per book in Canada.* I understand that accepting the 2 free books and gifts places me under no obligation to buy anything. I can always return a shipment and cancel at any time. Even if I never buy another book, the two free books and gifts are mine to keep forever.

240/340 HDN FEFR

Name	(PLEASE PRINT)	
Address		Apt. #
City	State/Prov.	Zip/Postal Code

Signature (if under 18, a parent or guardian must sign)

Mail to the **Reader Service:**
IN U.S.A.: P.O. Box 1867, Buffalo, NY 14240-1867
IN CANADA: P.O. Box 609, Fort Erie, Ontario L2A 5X3

Not valid for current subscribers to Harlequin Romantic Suspense books.

Want to try two free books from another line?
Call 1-800-873-8635 or visit www.ReaderService.com.

* Terms and prices subject to change without notice. Prices do not include applicable taxes. Sales tax applicable in N.Y. Canadian residents will be charged applicable taxes. Offer not valid in Quebec. This offer is limited to one order per household. All orders subject to credit approval. Credit or debit balances in a customer's account(s) may be offset by any other outstanding balance owed by or to the customer. Please allow 4 to 6 weeks for delivery. Offer available while quantities last.

Your Privacy—The Reader Service is committed to protecting your privacy. Our Privacy Policy is available online at www.ReaderService.com or upon request from the Reader Service.

We make a portion of our mailing list available to reputable third parties that offer products we believe may interest you. If you prefer that we not exchange your name with third parties, or if you wish to clarify or modify your communication preferences, please visit us at www.ReaderService.com/consumerschoice or write to us at Reader Service Preference Service, P.O. Box 9062, Buffalo, NY 14269. Include your complete name and address.

There was no way in hell he wanted the sheriff or any of the
deputies seeing Melanie in her sexy blue nightgown. He found
the white terry cloth robe just where she'd told him it would
be and carried it back into her bedroom with him. He helped
her into it and then wrapped his arms around her.

The idea that anyone would try to put their hands on her in
an effort to harm her shot rage through him.

"I didn't do this to myself," she whispered.

He leaned back and looked at her in surprise. "It never
crossed my mind that you did."

"Maybe somebody will think I'm just some poor crippled
woman looking for attention, that I tore the screen off the
window, left my wheelchair in the corner and then crawled
into the closet and waited for you to come home." A new sob
welled up and spilled from her lips.

"Melanie...stop," he protested.

She looked up at him with eyes that simmered with emotion. "Isn't that what you think? That I'm just a poor little cripple?"

"Never," he replied truthfully. "And you need to get that thought out of your head. We need to get you into the living room. The sheriff should be here anytime."

She swiped at the tears that had begun to fill her eyes once again. "Can you bring me my chair?"

He started for it and then halted in his tracks. "We need to leave it where it is. Maybe there are fingerprints on it that will let us know who was in here."

He walked back to where she sat on the bed and scooped her up in his arms. Once again, she wrapped her arms around his neck and leaned into him. For a moment he imagined that he could feel her heartbeat matching the rhythm of his own.

"It's going to be all right, Melanie," he promised. "I'm here and I'm going to make sure everything is all right." He just hoped it was a promise he could keep.

Will Melanie ride off into the sunset with her sexy new live-in cowboy? Or will a murderous lunatic, lurking just a breath away, add another victim to his tally? Find out what happens next in COWBOY WITH A CAUSE

Available January 2013 only from Harlequin Romantic Suspense wherever books are sold.

HRSEXP1212